THE EVERYTHING
I HAVE LOST

THE EVERYTHING I HAVE LOST

-SYLVIA ZÉLENY-

CINCO PUNTOS PRESS  EL PASO, TEXAS

FIRST EDITION
10 9 8 7 6 5 4 3 2 1

Library of Congress Cataloging-in-Publication Data

Names: Aguilar Zéleny, Sylvia, 1973- author.
Title: The everything I have lost / by Sylvia Zéleny.
Description: First edition. | El Paso, Texas : Cinco Puntos Press, [2019] | Summary: Beginning at age twelve, Julia keeps a diary of her life in Juárez, Mexico, where life is always dangerous, until she joins her aunt and grandmother in El Paso, Texas, and faces new challenges. Identifiers: LCCN 2018049009 | ISBN 9781947627178 (cloth : alk. paper) | ISBN 9781947627185 (pbk. : alk. paper)] ISBN 9781947627192 (ebook)
Subjects: | CYAC: Coming of age—Fiction. | Family life—Mexico—Fiction. | Friendship—Fiction. | Diaries—Fiction. | Immigrants—Fiction. | Mexico—Fiction. | El Paso (Tex.) —Fiction.
Classification: LCC PZ7.1.A325 Eve 2019 | DDC [Fic]—dc23
LC record available at https://lccn.loc.gov/2018049009

Book and cover design by BLUE PANDA STUDIOS
Author photo by CARLOS HERNANDEZ

A12007 388254

TO MY SON JUAN AND HIS EVERYTHING,
BECAUSE HE IS EVERYTHING.

oNE

"When you pick up a pen,
put it to paper and let yourself go,
certain words throw themselves at you…"

Sonja Livingston, *Ghostbread*

JANUARY 30TH

- A cherry-flavored lipstick.
- 50 pesos.
- Two boxes of Chiclets: mint and watermelon.
- A Hello Kitty wallet.
- A keychain that said, *I* ❤ *Texas* that Tía gave me.
- My old diary with three blank pages.

EVERYTHING. Everything that I had in my purse. Everything that was left in the car.

The CAR that was stolen.

We walked out of the movie theater and it was gone. Mamá asked Papá if he had forgotten where it was parked. We looked everywhere. But the car was nowhere to be found.

Mamá cried, *Our car, our car.* Willy didn't say anything, he kept quiet. He just looked at us like he was trying to understand, but not really. Willy doesn't really talk that much. He's like Papá. Quiet like a stone in the middle of nowhere. Papá, as always, he was just mad on the inside. But on the outside, well, you can never tell what he's like. Except when he drinks beer. He is all smiles when he drinks beer.

Papá took his phone and called someone. Papá and his commands, do this, do that. He said, Pick us up at the movie theatre. No, the car didn't break down. The car is gone. Yes, gone.

I am not surprised. This is becoming more and more common here. Juárez is becoming the city that steals cars, girls, *and our dignity*, my teacher says. I wonder what dignity looks like. All I can think about is my purse, my lipstick, the pesos, my gum, my diary, my *I* ♥ *Texas* keychain. From now on we will have to wake up earlier, we will have to start keeping coins in our pockets, we will have to take the bus, I hate the bus. It's embarrassing to take the bus.

It sucks, it really really really sucks. We were just getting used to it. I look out the window, I hate this city, I don't know why we came to live here, I still can't get used to it. All I can think of is my things.

FEBRUARY 2ND

Mamá gave me this new notebook with the words *Just Write*
on the cover. So: new diary, new writing, same girl. At first,
I wanted to rewrite everything I could remember, but then I
thought, what's the point? I will just share some basics and
move on.

I was born in El Paso, right over there—>. I can see it from
here, I see some buildings from my window. I lived there for like a
second, then we moved and moved and moved. I wish I could live
in El Paso, people say it is much better. I am sure it is, I am sure it is
way better than this or any of the cities Dad has made us live in. In
the last years we've moved a lot. Believe me, I can tell you anything
about Sinaloa, Sonora, Nuevo León and Tamaulipas. Tamaulipas,
isn't that a very nice word? In the news they say that in Tamaulipas
people steal cars and girls. And dignities, my teacher would add.

But I wonder if they also steal dignity there? In El Paso? I
have to ask the teacher what dignity really is, what it looks like.
Does dignity look different in every place you go?

FEBRUARY 23RD

Mamá took me to the dentist today. I hate the dentist. The place was packed, as if all the kids in the world had cavities at the same time: *a plague of plaque!* We sat and waited. Mamá read her book and I grabbed a magazine.

I read a phrase in it that I liked. I wrote it down so I wouldn't forget: *Kids and crazy people are allowed to speak the truth and to say the opposite at the same time.*

In this diary, I'm going to speak the truth *and* also say the opposite—

AT
THE
SAME
TIME!

FEBRUARY 27TH

I show some of my classmates my new diary. They say that no one writes in diaries anymore. They say that it's just for bored old ladies. I'm not bored or old. I write just because. They just don't get it, except for Tere. She says that writing in a diary must be like keeping a slice of everything.

SLICE,
SLICE,
SLICE.

Tere has never asked me to show her the inside of my diary. She just asks me what I write about. I go, Sometimes I write about what I see, do, hear, eat, drink, and smell. I write about whatever I want. Sometimes I observe everything that happens in the day and wait till nighttime to write it down, detail by tiny detail, by tiny detail, by...

She smiles. I tell her that sometimes my day is wasted and flat and I think there's nothing to write in my diary, but then I end up writing more than ever. Tere nods. Tere gets it.

I think there are stories that are not planned, they just come out. They come through your fingers at lightning speed and all of a sudden you can't stop writing. It's like someone dictated paragraphs of your life to you, and you are just trying to keep up.

I wonder what would happen if I didn't obey that voice and

didn't write. Would paragraphs haunt me in my sleep? I don't want paragraphs to haunt me, so I follow the voice. I follow *my* voice. When Mamá sees me writing she says, You remind me of me when I was a kid. Only she didn't write, she drew. Mamá is an artist, she draws, paints, takes photos, she sometimes teaches art to rich ladies and rich kids.

Tía told me once that Mamá could've been a famous artist. She can't be one no more? I asked her. Tía looked at me and said, Not with that father of yours. I don't know what she means, but it feels like one of those *better-not-ask* things.

Anyway, there are also things that you swear you will never write about, and you end up writing down each and every one. It's like something you can't avoid. You just write. Yes, there are *you-better-write-about-it* things. Like Tere, I better write about Tere.

MARCH 9TH

I have always been really bad at school, maybe because we moved a lot, and I was always the new girl. Or perhaps our moving has nothing to do with it, and I just suck at school. Who knows? Anyway, when I started going to school here in Juárez, the school year had already started, and everybody knew each other. And worse, everybody knew what was happening on the board. I would see letters or numbers, or letters AND numbers, and didn't understand a thing.

Two weeks after my arrival, examinations started. Mamá tried to convince them not to test me, not yet, but our teacher and the principal said that was the only way to see how I was doing. I asked, What if I fail, will you send me back to fifth grade? They said no, but I didn't believe them.

I was freaking out. The test came, and I did not know what to do. The first section was math. I was just as blank as the paper in front of me. Then this girl right next to me showed me her test, pointed out the answers with her pencil. Are you sure? I whispered. She nodded. That girl was Tere.

I'm gonna be honest, I did copy many things from her test, but some others I answered on my own, maybe seeing her stuff made me remember this and that. She gave me confidence. She still does, and that is why she is my best friend.

Tere was once the new girl at school, and she too came from another city to live here, so she knew what it felt like to not know a thing about anything.

Sometimes we hang out with the rest of the girls at school,

but mostly it is us, only us. We don't need anybody else. We sit down, share our lunch and talk about our favorite TV shows and our favorite singers and about the other girls and clothes and shoes

AND...

AND...

AND...

MARCH 19TH

This is Willy, he is six, and this is Julia, she is twelve, Mamá says to the nurse who will give us shots, and…

I interrupt Mamá and correct her: I am almost thirteen. Thirteen.

I can see Mamá and the nurse sharing a look like they want to laugh at me, but they don't dare. The nurse says, Thirteen, wow, you are almost a teenager. Then she takes Willy and sits him on the table, she cleans his arm and says, This won't hurt a bit. Willy looks at Mamá, like he's begging for mercy. It is OK, Mamá says, you will get candy later.

Then it is my turn. The nurse says, Well, since you are ALMOST thirteen, this will be your last shot ever. I feel important. I ask Mamá if this is true. Yes, she says. This is your last shot ever. The nurse cleans my arm and then she asks, So tell me, now that you are almost thirteen, do you have a boyfriend and everything? I shake my head. Are you sure? I wanna say, Believe me, lady, if I had a boyfriend everyone would know, but instead, I shake my head and smile. She gives me the shot and my smile disappears. It sucks to be almost thirteen, but still stuck at twelve, cause you gotta look old and yelling or crying is out of the question.

MARCH 30TH

Papá has a new job and he's going to make **A LOT** of money, that's what he said today at dinner. I went with el Gringo, he told Mamá, I'm in. I will get a car and everything. Mamá didn't reply. Papá asked Willy and me if we were happy that he had a job. We both said yes. I am the happiest because having a car means we won't have to ride the bus again.

I really really really hate the bus. It's always so crowded, and people who ride it have big bags and luggage and many of them stink. Mom says that it is because they are going to El Paso or coming from El Paso and they walk to and from the bridge. And what's in their bags? I ask her. Treasures, she says. Mom says that people bring treasures for their families here to Juárez, or they take treasures to their families in El Paso. But what kind of treasures? I want to know. Mom first shrugs, then says, Think of what your auntie brings you when she visits us. I close my eyes and I see:

- Chocolates
- Peanut butter
- Bread, lots of bread, the one with nuts
- Boxes and boxes of macaroni and cheese
- Chips in a can

Tía and Bis come every other weekend to visit from El Paso. They bring stuff for all of us: food, shoes, toys, stickers. And when they leave they take tortillas, bread, chile colorado, and cheese that they buy from the market downtown. I guess there's no tortillas, bread or cheese over there.

Anyway, once Papá gets this other car, we won't have to ride in the bus squished by bags that smell like soap or chorizo. If everything goes well, he will buy one for Mom by Christmas. Papá says that things are looking good for him, and luckily we won't have to move again in a very long time. Mamá insists, We should try to move to El Paso, maybe you can get a job there. Papá says that maybe it's not a bad idea to move to El Paso, but he doesn't need a job because he works with el Gringo.

Mamá makes a face, it's like she doesn't like this el Gringo. I can't help it. I ask, Who is el Gringo?

Mamá just stares at Papá. She has her see-I-told-you-so face. Then she insists, We could live in El Paso. If you get your visa, there would be no need to work for this guy.

Dad says nothing.

Mamá was born in El Paso, Willy and me were also born there too. Many kids in Juárez are born there, then brought here. Papá was born in Mexico. Bis doesn't like Papá all that much. She says he is a bit of an ass.

I like it when adults say words like ass, balls, shit or the F-word. Especially the F-word. One day I will write the F-word with bold capital letters. I think the F-word is kinda cool. And pinche, I love pinche. I never use pinche.

Papá uses that word a lot. He uses it the way other people use salt or sugar. If he's mad, he uses it a lot. If he's not mad, he uses it just sometimes. Pinche this, pinche that.

APRIL 1ST

Mamá doesn't let us go outside. We don't do it, but we always
want to, especially now that we're on summer vacation. No, no,
Mamá says, the street is not a safe place. Come on, I tell her, we
will just be right outside the house.

Mamá: No.

I try again, this time I use my brother. Willy REALLY wants
to play outside, Mamá. Come on.

No and no.

She opens the curtain and shows me the street. Do you
see anyone playing outside? she asks. She is right. There isn't
anyone playing outside. The only ones playing on the streets
from time to time are dogs or cats.

Willy pulls my sleeve and tells me to just go to our
backyard. So we do.

He takes one of his Lego figures, and I bring my diary, but
Mamá tells me to leave it behind and play with my brother. Our
backyard is super small. I don't even remember when the last
time was when I came out. The walls are higher than before.
This is a fortress made of concrete and glass, lots of broken
glass on top of it all.

After a while, I tell Willy we should just go inside and
watch TV.

On TV we watch kids balance on top of walls like the ones
in our backyard, like gymnasts. Up they go. We could never do
it here, not on our walls, not on anyone else's walls, because

all the walls here have broken glass. All the houses here are concrete fortresses.

It is really no fun to play in a fortress.

APRIL 5TH

Tell your mother to go to church today, it's the third anniversary of the Pope's death. It was my tía on the phone. Tía was all drama and emotions.

Who? I asked.

The Pope, the Pope, our John Paul II. Tía sounded like she was about to cry, as if this Pope was an uncle, a cousin, or the dog she loved the most.

Mamá came over to the phone, What's going on?

I reported: the Pope died and my tía is crying.

He died a long time ago and she's still in mourning, oh my god! Mamá said, rolling her eyes like she does when we do something really really stupid. Mamá takes the phone and does what she does best: she calms people's worries. Like when the neighbor's daughter disappeared. Like when a kid at her school was killed by a stray bullet. Like when we woke up to find a dog had been killed in front of the house. There are a few more *like whens* but I don't want to think about them right now.

When Mamá hangs up with Tía, I ask, How did this guy die? Was he shot in the street? Did they light him on fire? Was he kidnapped? How did it go down?

Shut up, Mamá says, you don't know what you are talking about.

But I do. I know. I know everything. We all do, because it's on TV, on the radio, in the headlines of the newspaper we never buy, but that I leaf through at the corner store. People don't just die, people get shot, set on fire or kidnapped.

APRIL 17TH

So, a few weeks ago we got a new car, and now—now, you won't believe this—we got a **NEW HOUSE**. A brand new house.

Of all the houses we have lived in, this is the one I like the most. I like it because I don't have to share a room with Willy. I have my own bedroom, and Mamá put in a desk for me so I can do my homework and write in my diary. I like it because there are two bathrooms. I like it because we have a huge yard, way better than the old one, and this is where Willy and I play our games. Yes, I know I am too old to play games with my little brother, but what else can I do? Mamá still does not let us play outside or become friends with our neighbors, and she doesn't let me go hang out with Tere all that much.

Willy and me, we like to play war. That's what every kid plays here anyway. You see them in the streets with pretend machine guns shooting everywhere. We do the same. We shoot at everything, we shoot at the wall, we shoot at our toys, we shoot at the plants Mamá keeps on the patio so they get sun. (Yes, we kill plants.)

Willy says he misses the old house, he says he liked it better, but that is only because he got to sleep with me, **DUH**. I tell him that he just has to get used to it, which is what Papá says to Mamá every time we move.

I like that this house has bars all over the place. I feel safe in it. Yes, this house makes me happy and makes me safe.

MAY 23RD

I haven't been writing a lot, sometimes I feel I have nothing to write about. But Bis is here and I am sure she will give me a lot of material. Bis came to spend the summer with us… She and my aunt cross the bridge very often, but sometimes not so often. Sometimes, not at all. But now they are here, and Bis is here and she is staying for the rest of the summer.

Bis always, always, always brings gifts for Willy and me. She fills our pantry. That means we are going to eat my favorite: mac & cheese (the blue box ones) or spaghetti (in the red can). While everyone was helping to get the stuff out of my tía's car, I took Bis to my room and showed her the room and my beautiful desk.

Bis sat on my bed and asked, Is this where you will be doing your homework?

Yes, but it's also where I will become an author. I will write children's stories. Mamá wants me to draw and paint like her and…

Bis interrupted me. Yeah, but we already have an artist. Now we need an author, right?

My thoughts exactly.

Bis always understands me. She knows that I am happy / not happy that school's over.

JUNE 3RD

Willy asked Bis today why we call her Bis. Is that your real name? he asked.

She said, No, my name is Julia, like your sister, but I am your bisabuela, and bisabuela is too long of a word.

Bisabuela? What is a bisabuela? Willy asked.

The mother of your grandma, I said.

So, you are not our grandma? Willy asked surprised.

No, I am not, I am your great-grandma.

OK, he said and he went back to watching TV.

It had never occurred to me that my bis is my bis because there is a grandma, but where's the grandma? I asked her, Bis, where is grandma? Bis shrugged and continued watching Willy's show.

Bis, Bis, Bis, I said, Bis, where is grandma?

Bis shushed me and said, I will tell you all about her when you are a bit older.

But I am almost thirteen, I said.

JUNE 7TH

Last night we were awakened by gunfire.

Well, it only woke up Mamá, Papá, and me. Willy and Bis had no idea. It sounded really close. I can't remember what I was dreaming, but the sound of the bullets came into my dream and pulled me out of it. I woke up terrified. I sat there for a bit wondering if it had been a nightmare. Then I heard the shots again and went to my parent's room.

Papá was on his feet, alert. He had a pistol in his hand. Mamá had her hands over her mouth. Papá motioned *shhhhhhhh* with his finger and left the room. He locked the other deadbolt on the kitchen door. The loud clack freaked me out. When he came back, I was hugging my mom. Both of us were super scared. He told me I could go to bed now, he promised everything was going to be okay.

As I was leaving, I stopped to ask, Have you always had a gun?

He didn't answer.

Unless half-smiles are answers of some sort.

I went back to bed.

As I walked to my room, I repeated under my breath, Everything is going to be okay. Papá has a pistol, everything is going to be okay. He is strong, and he'll protect us. If someone gets into the house, Papá will kill him. Like this: pow pow, two shots, that's it. We are lucky. So lucky.

Nothing can happen to us, not even here, in this city where gunfire rings out at night.

I like it when Bis is with us. I like it because it means that in the afternoons when Mamá has to go out, we can stay with Bis. Bis will take care of us, even though Mom tells us that we are the ones to take care of her.

Willy plays with his game and while he kills zombies, Bis and I watch a soap: *Amor en Custodia*. In today's episode, Paz is almost kidnapped.

Kidnapped is like when the boogeyman takes you away, right? I ask Bis. She looks at me like I am asking where babies come from. She nods.

I ask why they do it.

Well, they just do, to make money, dear.

During the commercials we go to the kitchen and make ourselves some toast with jelly. She asks if I know anything about my Papá's new job. I say that it's with some guy called el Gringo and that he will make a lot of money.

Of course he will, she said.

Bis doesn't like Papá very much, but she must really not like his boss because she says, Ese pinche Gringo.

It's all the same to me, we have a new car and I don't have to go back to that stinky bus and we have this new house and…

More like a new jail, says Bis pointing at bars on the windows.

You don't like our house? I ask her.

Bis shrugs, then says, What I don't like is what your parents have decided for their lives, and yours.

I don't understand her, but who cares. I just love it when Bis is here.

JUNE 16TH

We were riding in Papá's new car. The five of us. Willy was Papá's copilot, and Mamá was sitting in the backseat with Bis and me. We were waiting at a stop sign, music playing on the radio. All of a sudden a car started shooting at another car right across from us.

PUM PUM!

I just remember that Mamá and Bis covered me with their bodies. Papá drove away real fast. Then hit the brakes.

Is everyone okay?

We were all okay.

Who did they kill, who did they kill? Willy asked.

What happened to you? Mamá said to Willy. My brother had some blood on his forehead. Both my parents went all crazy about it, but it was a scratch, just a scratch.

Mamá looked at Papá and said, Let's go home.

The very next day I told Tere all about it on the phone. See, Tere, we were at a stop sign, then we hear **PUM PUM,** then...

Everything went back to normal, right? she added. Tere says this happens very often in the neighborhood she and her mom used to live in. She has already seen three dead bodies. You get used to it. It's OK. There's shooting everywhere.

She is right. Lately, there is shooting everywhere.

Everywhere.

During dinner, I tell everyone what Tere said. I tell them, It's OK. There's shooting everywhere.

Mamá says, It's not OK. We must be more careful, we must...

Papá interrupts her and says, There is nothing we can do about it. It is what it is.

Next time, says Willy, I will bring my rifle, and I will shoot at everyone who tries to scare us.

JUNE 22ND

There was a loud sound of cans being thrown into the garbage. It was Bis. She was throwing away a lot of tomato puree cans. What are you doing, Nana? Mamá asked her, but Bis just shrugged and continued making coffee, putting cinnamon sticks in like always. I love the smell of coffee with cinnamon.

She poured a cup for herself and let me sip when Mamá wasn't looking. Then, all of a sudden, she stood up and started opening all the cabinet doors from the kitchen as if she was searching for something.

What is it? Mamá asked her.

I am looking for the cinnamon, she said.

It's here, and you already made the coffee with it, remember, Nana?

Nana. That is how Mamá calls Bis.

I had never thought about it.

I tried all day to find the perfect moment to ask Mamá why she calls her Nana and not Grandma.

Finally, after dinner, while she was working in her little studio, I asked her. You know, she said, it is one of those silly things about your bis. She believed Grandmother and Grandma were names that made her look old. Your tía and I used to call her Grandma, you know? But when we moved in with her, after our mother left, she trained us to call her Nana. And that's what we've been calling her ever since.

She says it just like that—*my mother left*.

The big secret is out, and she probably doesn't realize it.

I tried my luck and asked her. She left you? Your mother left you? Mamá looked at me, straight into my eyes. I thought she was gonna send me to brush my teeth and go to bed, but she didn't.

Yes, she left, my mother left your tía and me when we were kids.

Question after question came out of my mouth. It was as if words were just waiting for a chance to come out. Why did she leave? How old were you? Do you miss her? Did you never see her again? What about your dad? Do you have a dad? Seriously, where's your mother? Do you miss her?

But I had lost Mamá without noticing. She went back to working on a landscape as my questions flew around her like flies. I looked at her canvas. There was a mountain. The rain was coming. Mamá was somewhere in there.

I was about to leave the room when Mamá said, I don't miss her. Nana is the mother that anyone would want and we are lucky to have her. Calling her Grandma would not be enough, she is not like any other grandma. Now that I think about it, calling her Nana makes it more special.

Mamá went on talking about Bis, but I got stuck with the idea of her mother leaving two little girls, just like that.

Right now I can't sleep just thinking about it. I know that fathers often leave, but mothers? Mothers can't leave, they are the thing that glues a family together.

Mamá glues us.

If I were a bit younger I would go to her bed and cuddle with her. I would glue myself to her. I know she will never leave, but still…

JULY 5TH

Julia, I got my period, Tere says as soon as she gets on the phone. It takes me like forever to grasp her words. You did? I say. Yes, she answers, I got **MY PERIOD, MY PE-RI-ID**. My period, she repeats, as if she is rubbing it in the world's face or just mine because she knows I haven't gotten mine. If I had gotten mine already, she and everyone would know because I would be doing exactly the same, yelling **I GOT MY PERIOD, I GOT MY PERIOD**.

We've been waiting for it, we've been talking about it for ages. OK, maybe not ages, maybe just this last year. But it is a big deal and we both know it and now she got it and I haven't.

I am nothing. She is everything.

Tía is here. She says she came to visit us, but we all know she came to take Bis back. Bis lives with her in El Paso. I like Tía, she is funny. She spills the beans about everything very easily. I just hate that when she is here, we have to go to church.

Church is her favorite subject. Tía talks too much about church. Today for example she was talking about it being the year of the Eucharist.

The year of Eu-what? asked Willy.

Eu-cha-rist, she repeated.

You wouldn't understand, I told him.

The truth is that I don't understand it either, but I acted like I did. I do that a lot with my family, with Tere. I hate being seen as the one who knows nothing. I know how to play smart, a couple of nods, a serious look.

Me, I don't like to go to church, it smells like candles, like dust, like old people, like death. I've never smelled a dead person, but I'm sure it smells like church—an ugly, foul odor.

Church freaks me out a bit. The last time we went, for example, the priest had us pray for the safety of our city and for the souls of the people that we lose every day and all the women were in tears.

How do you lose a soul?

Bis says that it is kinda funny that this is the year of the Eucharist because this is actually the Chinese Year of the Dog. It makes me laugh. The year of the dog, I repeat. Willy barks and barks.

Tía gets mad.

Tía always gets mad and when she gets mad, she makes the ugliest face.

JULY 7TH, VERY LATE. EVERYONE'S SLEEPING.

I wonder how it feels to have a sister. I look at Mamá and Tía when they talk and laugh and touch each other's hands or laps like they do, and I feel jealous. I wish I had a sister. Wait, that does not mean I don't love my baby brother. No, I love him so much it hurts me to see him cry every time he falls or every time Papá leaves and Willy cries a river.

But.

I wish I had a sister. I know I have Tere and she is like a sister to me, but I wish I had an **OLDER** sister. I wish I had a sister that would teach me all about boys and bras and hair and everything that has to do with being a girl.

It is **SO** hard being a girl.

Mamá sometimes explains stuff, but I feel that she leaves out some details. Like when she explained about girls having their period. She wouldn't tell me why. Why do we get our period?

Tía is older than Mamá, and I guess that means she knows more because every once in a while when Mamá confides something Tía says, I told you so. I need an I-told-you-so sister, so I can become an I-told-you-so to Willy, but really there are few chances for me to tell him so, I am not that smart.

But just like I want an older sister, Tía wants a daughter. She wants a daughter just like me. She says that all the time. Tía has a son named Jonás, but he never comes to Juárez. He doesn't like it, she says, so I haven't seen him in ages.

Tía says, You and Jonás used to play a lot when you were

little kids, he was like an older brother to you. But I don't remember. I don't remember what it feels like to have a cousin that is like an older brother. I wonder if he ever said I told you so to me.

JULY 9TH

Bis reads the tarot cards.

Tía says that is as bad as talking to the devil.

Bis has told me not to believe in the devil. It is people who are the devil, she says.

Anyway, Mamá's friends sometimes come when Bis is here and say, Doña Julia, can you read the tarot cards for me?

Bis says that before the actual reading, one has to call the tarot guardians. I don't see them, but I believe they are there, right behind her. I know there are many other things we cannot see that hide somewhere around us.

I wanna learn to read the tarot. Can you imagine? I could be so popular in school. Every girl and boy would surround me, asking me to do a reading for them. I would wear my hair up and a lot of jewelry, my nails would be long and red. I would need a name, a fantastic magical name. Bis says my card is The Star. In French, it's called Le Toille.

The card is kinda weird.

The mouth on her belly button makes me laugh, but what I like about it is that instead of taking water from the river, she is putting water into the river.

The star is a giver, Bis says.

I am a giver.

JULY 12TH

Sometimes I hate Mamá. I hate her so much. Today, for example, I hated her from when I woke up until it got dark. See, yesterday we went shopping and I asked her to buy me a lipstick, but a real one. A lipstick that does not taste like bubblegum or watermelon or strawberry, I said.

Mamá said a big no.

Come on, I said, I want a real lipstick, a pink or red or plum-colored lipstick.

No, you are too young.

But I am not, I said.

Yes, you are.

No, no, I am not, I am almost thirteen and all the girls my age already wear lipstick.

And do you know how they end up? Mamá said. No daughter of mine will be wearing makeup as if she was a puta.

A puta, a whore, that's what she said, angry as I hadn't seen her in a while.

Everything around us stopped, everyone around us just stood waiting for more action to happen. Or maybe it just seemed that way to me, like we were a soap opera for everybody to watch.

A soap opera with very bad acting.

We didn't talk on the way home. We didn't talk at dinner. We pretended that we didn't exist for each other.

I hate her. I **HATE** her. It's like she wants me to live in a bubble.

JULY 15TH

One of Mamá's friends came with her daughter from Aguascalientes to do whoknowswhat with their papers because her husband is on the other side. They are staying with us for a couple of days. They will sleep in my room, and I will sleep in Willy's room. We don't ever have visitors like these, ones that aren't family.

Papá doesn't like Leticia, that's the name of Mamá's friend. Papá says she's a busybody. Papá's right. Leticia asks Mamá the price of everything we own. She's all, These cabinets are so pretty, how much did they cost? Your sandals are so cute, how much did they cost? And the worst, Why do you live here and not over there, can't you live over there, if you have your papers?

Leticia is very *opinionated*. You don't get nervous with Guillermo traveling so much, with everything going on around here? she asks. You aren't scared to stay all alone with the kids with everything that's going on around here? You aren't scared of everything going on around here?

Everything going on around here is everythingthatsgoingoninthiscountry.

Leticia's daughter is just like her. Her name is Tina and just this morning she told me, Here's where the dead women are, right? You didn't know any of them? They say sometimes they only find their skeletons.

I didn't answer her yes or no, I just made the gesture you

make so other people think you get it, even when you don't.
You know, tight lips, looking down, shrugging my shoulders.
Besides, I didn't know what "skeletons" meant. I mean, a
skeleton is just a bone, isn't it?

I looked it up in the dictionary:

skeleton.
- n. the structure of bones that supports the body of a man or
  animal

- n. a set or model of all the bones in a man's body

Skeletons are not just a bone, they are a body, a whole
body. Skeletons are us. Are skeletons for women too or just for
men and animals? And, anyway, what do they do to the dead
women of Juárez so that only their skeletons remain?

Also, who is **THEY**?

I called Tere on the phone. Can you believe that classes don't start for another month? I said.

It's like summer lasts a lifetime, she said.

I told Tere that I've been watching *Amor en Custodia* this week and she said that it was a re-run, she said she used to watch it with her mom last year. Tere is always ahead of everything. She says that her mom likes those realistic shows.

Realistic? I asked her.

You know, the ones that tell the truth about people and the things that are going on in this country. She said that as if she had all the answers: *The things that are going on in this country.* Then she went, You know?

Yup, I said.

Hey, I said, have you heard about this thing that happens to the women of Juárez, how is it called?

Las muertas de Juárez, Tere says.

Tere is a know-it-all. **FUCKING TERE**.

I know I'm not supposed to use the F-word, but I don't care.

Yes, I have heard of them, everybody has. Why?

Someone asked me about it, I said.

Yeah, said Tere, everybody wants to know about them.

I told Tere about Tina. I told her how she has an opinion about everything, just like her mom. I told her how she gets to wear lipstick and eyeliner when we go out, and her mother says nothing.

She's not gonna be your new best friend, right?

Of course not, I answered, and I meant it. There is no way this girl could be my friend. She doesn't understand a thing about us and about our life. Plus, she keeps saying she hates it here and how she could never live on the border.

Why doesn't she like the border? Tere asked.

I told her what the girl said, her exact words: Because my mom says the border is like being at the edge all the time and normal people don't like being on the edge. Do you think we live on the edge? I asked Tere.

I don't know, she said, but now I don't like that girl either.

Papá has started to travel a lot.

He's been gone three days now and Mamá is all restless, I can tell because she calls him more than five times a day and doesn't want to go out. To make things worse, her friend keeps saying that Papá should not leave that often considering the way things are here.

What does she mean by that? I wonder.

This time Papá went to Tijuana. He leaves a lot—A LOT—of money when he goes away, but we don't spend it because, as I said, Mamá doesn't go out when he is gone. Instead, she stuffs the bills into a sock and then puts it back into the drawer.

Mamá's friend said that in Tijuana things are real hot. I don't know what this means. Real hot? I'm not stupid, I know she's not saying hot-watch-out-you're-going-to-burn-yourself, so then what does it mean?

I go to the dictionary:

hot.

- adj. Having or producing heat.
- adj. Said of a room, a garment, etc.: They provide warmth and comfort.
- adj. Said of a dispute, an argument, or a fight, etc.: Heated, lively.
- adj. Conflicted, problematic. Tensions rise for a hot autumn.

Hot like difficult, like real complicated. Papá is very strong, and besides he has a gun so nothing's going to happen to him even though things in Tijuana are *real hot.*

Before moving here Papá considered living in Tijuana.

I remember their conversation, it went like this:

Papá: We should move to Tijuana.

Mamá: No way, José.

(OK, probably she didn't say THAT, but you get the idea)

Papá: Tijuana is better than Juárez, there are more opportunities.

Mamá: Maybe, but my family lives in El Paso, and we could be close to them.

Papá: Your family doesn't like me.

Mamá: But I do.

And then they probably kissed, Mamá and Papá are always kissing.

Tere told me once that Tijuana and Juárez were very similar anyway. And is that good? I asked.

And bad too, she said.

JULY 30TH

Finally, Mamá's friend and her pinche daughter left. They were here almost **TWO WEEKS**. Before them, I never said pinche. Before them I said stupid, idiot, dumb, everything but pinche. OK, I said the F-word once. But with her I learned to say pinche, and I finally understood what pinche exactly meant, and I know what it is to be a pinche.

And she is really **PINCHE** because:

1. She told me that if I didn't wear a bra, my boobies were never going to grow, that men like boobies and that if you don't have boobies, no one will like you.
2. She told me that one day I was going to have so much hair down there, it would gross me out to pee.
3. She told me that if I didn't learn to take care of myself, I was going to end up like all the girls who disappeared and never came back.
4. She told me that if I didn't get my act together, an old man was going to take me away.

Mamá says that pinche girl told me all that because she's just envious, because she likes my things my room my shoes my clothes my family my my my my my *everything*!

Mamá says that pinche girl's mom is the same way. It's envy, pure envy because we finally have what we've always wanted.

AUGUST 1ST

Mamá says you shouldn't look at or listen to or read the news. But she can't stop looking at or listening to or reading the news. Especially now that Papá is always away. For example, this morning we ate breakfast while we watched the news about a hurricane in the United States. A hurricane with the name of a woman. A hurricane with the name of a doll. We watched people crying, we watched the wind blowing, and water water water everywhere, the houses torn to pieces.

Poor families, Mamá repeated over and over.

There are houses like that here, I told Mamá. We hardly go over there, but I've seen them, right there on top of the mountain, next to where it says LA BIBLIA ES LA VERDAD, LEÉLA.

There are poor families and people crying and empty houses everywhere…not just on the TV. I tell her that's what my teacher told us in school.

Mamá doesn't say anything. Lately, it's like she's there but not. She can be right next to you and still you miss her as if she wasn't. I miss Mamá, I miss her like those kids who probably miss their big, dry houses.

AUGUST 12TH

Tere called me today.
 We were on the phone for hours.

H O U R S!

AUGUST 14TH

It's been raining a lot.

Papá's still gone and Mamá doesn't like when it rains. Actually, Mamá doesn't like anything when Papá is not here.

She calls us to her room and she tells us to sleep there so the thunder doesn't scare us. But thunder doesn't scare anyone more than it does Mamá. She says that thunderbolts sound like gunshots.

Bis taught us long ago to scream real loud right after the thunder, that's how you get rid of fear, she said. Scream! Screaming loud will get rid of your fear of everything, I tell Mamá, but she doesn't scream. At least let us do it before we go crazy, Mamá. She scolds us and says we make her nervous and we are giving her a headache.

Mamá always has a headache.

It's easy to predict thunder. First you see one lightning bolt, sometimes another, then **BOOM** thunder. There's small thunder, medium thunder, large thunder. Willy says it would be nice to catch it and keep it in a box then take it out to scare people like one would keep lizards. A thunder is like if everything in the sky came together and said, **PINCHE**. Is a thunder as strong as a gunshot? I ask Mamá. Where do you come up with these things, Julia? she asks, but doesn't answer *my* question.

We huddle together and wait for the lightning, the thunder, the scream that's going to come out of us.

Kids, you are giving me a headache, she says.

No, we are not, you already had one, I say.

AUGUST 18TH

The rain is gone, and it left a mess. As if the city wasn't already a mess itself, Mamá says. Our yard is flooded, so I can't take Willy out to play. He is bored, so bored that he is all over Mamá and she asks me to entertain him.

This is what I did, I gave him a notebook and told him to start a diary, just like me. I am not that very good at writing, he says. Then just draw, but stop complaining, I said. I sounded like Mamá. You are no boss of mine, Willy said. He sounded like Papá. But then I gave him the look, the look Mamá has given to me so many times that I know now how to do it, and he stopped.

So here we are now, no rain, but still locked up. It feels like we have been locked up the whole summer. I can't believe I am saying this, but I am ready for school to start

AUGUST 22ND

Papá is back and today we all went shopping for school supplies. The new school year starts next week. They gave us this list:

- Pencils, three
- Pencil eraser
- A box of colored pencils, <u>NO CRAYONS OR MARKERS</u> (This looks suspicious, the capital letters, the underlining)
- Four packages of Play-Doh: yellow, blue, red, & green
- One package of Bond paper (like James Bond?)
- A ruler and a compass
- A glue stick
- Toilet paper, the school doesn't provide toilet paper in the student bathrooms. (Hopefully everyone buys the softest kind.)
- Feminine pads. (I asked Mamá, Why do we need this and if they are different from Masculine pads. She said those do not exist and that we have already talked about this, but I don't remember.)
- Spiral notebooks, two with graph paper and two double-lined wide
- Homework booklet (pinche homework)
- Yellow highlighter (and the pink? and the blue?)
- Cups/cones for the water cooler

SEPTEMBER 1ST

I don't know where Tere gets all this. Today she was telling me about this woman called la Mataviejitas, the Old Lady Killer. This lady pretends to be an old-people nurse, only she isn't for reals because she steals everything from them and then…and then she kills them.

I didn't believe her. How does she do that? Tere looked at me like I was an idiot and said, With her bare hands! And she put her hands around my neck.

She pulled a newspaper out of her backpack and showed me what the Mataviejitas looks like.

I can't believe someone would really kill old ladies.

I worry about my Bis.

I called her and told her, Don't get sick, Bis. Don't you ever hire someone to take care of you!

She says, I cannot not get sick. Everybody can get sick, baby.

I told her, OK, you can get sick, but please please please do not hire a nurse whenever you feel sick, especially a nurse you don't know. If you know her, that's fine, but if you don't, don't.

Bis said, Sometimes it is those you think you know the most who you should fear.

I didn't understand her. I said nothing.

But you have nothing to worry about, baby, she told me. This is the Year of the Dog, nothing bad can happen in the Year of the Dog.

I could hear my tía in the back saying, This is the year of

the Eucharist, not the Year of the Dog. Ay, Nana, how many times have I…

SEPTEMBER 1ST, VERY LATE

It's night. I am in my bed. I just woke up from a nightmare. I had a Mataviejitas nightmare. I dreamt that she got close to my bis and that there's no one but me to defend her, but then the Mataviejitas tries to kill me even though I am just a girl.

In my dream, the Mataviejitas turned into the Mataniñitas.

SEPTEMBER 3RD

The kids at school say that the people who kill women here also kill girls. So—there are actual people who are Mataniñitas.

If you think about it too much, it is even scarier.

SEPTEMBER 4TH

I
am
turning
THIRTEEN
in a week.

A WEEEEEEK.

SEPTEMBER 11TH

It's our third week of school. My social studies teacher is nice though she sometimes talks too much. She uses her family as an example for everything. She talks a lot about our responsibility as *Mexicanos* and stuff. She told us, on our very first day of classes, to always share with her all our good news, because a social studies class always needs good news. What kind of good news? someone asked. Birthdays, for example, she said.

Today, after passing out the list, I raise my hand.

Yes, Julia.

Today is my birthday. I smile.

Today? This exact day? she asks.

I smile and nod yes. She lowers her head. She leaves the chalk at the chalkboard and moves a little closer to us.

Today is a special day, she begins to say, and I think she is going to talk about me and tell everyone to sing las mañanitas or happy birthday to you and afterwards everyone will clap and give me hugs.

Children, on this day, a couple of years ago, the most terrible act of terrorism ever committed was carried out against our neighbors in the United States. The Twin Towers, symbols of New York City, were brought down. Today is a day to think, to reflect, on how fortunate we are.

After a long pause, the teacher says to me, Julia, since your birthday falls on an important date, you must celebrate life.

So, there were no mañanitas or happy birthdays to you, there was no clapping no hugs no nothing. We spent the morning talking about stressed and unstressed syllables. Stressed and unstressed and stressed and unstressed and stressed and unstressed.

Later, at home, I ask my Mamá about the towers, the ones that fell on my birthday. My Mamá got sad. You seriously wanna talk about this?

Yes.

Mamá says, Two planes…

Mamá's story about the towers is sadder than what it says in Wikipedia. She told me that a group of guys, who are called terrorists, forced the pilots of two planes to fly into buildings

What do you mean fly into buildings?

She raised her palm vertically, like this. Then she flew her other hand horizontally, like this, and she showed me how it happened. Both her hands then landed onto her lap.

What happened to the passengers? What happened to the people in the building? What happened to the pilots?

Gone, all gone.

I don't want mañanitas or birthdays or anything anymore.

SEPTEMBER 12TH

Being thirteen is the same as being twelve. Maybe when you turn fourteen, or fifteen, there is an actual difference.

Or maybe not.

SEPTEMBER 14TH

Mamá has started teaching drawing classes at a private school. In the past she did a course or two once in a while, but now, now she is all fancy.

I don't know exactly what Mamá teaches her students because she makes the weirdest paintings. Her studio is also the laundry room, or was going to be the laundry room. Sometimes Mamá doesn't use paintbrushes, she uses her fingers. Mamá's fingers are a rainbow. I like to watch her when she paints, I like the way she moves her left leg while doing it, it's like she uses her entire body when she paints. Mamá's painting a dance.

But I never understand what she paints because

1. Mamá doesn't paint people or animals or trees or flowers.
2. There isn't one sun in any of her paintings.

Mamá paints what she feels and what she sees happening in the city, she says. And what Mamá feels and what she sees happening in the city is made of dark colors.

There is too much dark in Mamá.

Too much dark.

SEPTEMBER 15TH

Our math teacher missed classes today, and we did not have a sub, so someone from the principal's office sat in and let us do whatever we wanted. We started talking about this and that, you know, about the shows we like, the music we like, and about our families.

We also talked about Independence Day, which is tomorrow. Tere says that it is her favorite day because people yell **VIVA MÉXICO**. Some of my classmates say that there are big celebrations downtown. But we have never gone, or if we have, I don't remember.

Downtown is not safe anymore, not even to go yell *Viva México*. Anyway, they were talking about what it feels to be Mexican.

When I told everyone that I was an American citizen, they couldn't believe it. I felt important because some of my classmates have visas and some of them don't. Actually, MANY of them don't.

Like Tere. She doesn't have a visa, and she says she'll never have one. They won't give me one because of my dad, she says.

I don't know what exactly happened to her dad, but whenever something happens at her house, whenever she misses school, she always says: It was because of my dad. I know that I could ask her and I know that she'd tell me (Tere tells me everything). But I don't ask her, I know better.

So, when Tere tells us that she doesn't have a visa because of her dad, no one asks her even though I am sure we all wanna know about it. We can all guess that it must be a sad story, and no one likes sad stories.

SEPTEMBER 18TH

One of the kids in my class drew a picture with guns and people fighting and airplanes and kids running. I am not that great copying someone else's artwork, but since I couldn't stop thinking about it, I drew one for myself. His probably had more dead people. I can't stop looking at it. I don't like it. It makes me think about so many things.

SEPTEMBER 19TH

Papá's been coming and going way more than usual. Yesterday he got back from another one of his trips. He looked sad and tired, like he was empty. Mamá asked him, What's wrong? He said, This job is heavier than I thought. Mamá touched his arm and said, Well, leave it! We'll figure something else out. You don't have to do it, you…

Papá pushed her hand away. Right away, Mamá brought up her idea again of him getting a visa so we can all move to El Paso.

Mamá told him the same things she says when the topic is El Paso:

- There are more opportunities there
- There is more money
- It is safer
- It would be much better for us

But this time she adds a new one:

- Once there, we could get married

Get married? I asked. Aren't you **ALREADY** married?

So, it seems that my parents *are* married, but in order for things to work out in El Paso, they would need to marry there too. I don't understand all that very well, but it seems that even though Papá liked the idea at first he then realized that in order to do all that—get married, get his papers—they would need a lot of money and the only way for him to get more money is to continue doing all this work and traveling for el Gringo, his boss.

Plus, Papá said, he won't let me go that easy.

I asked him what he meant, but then Mamá got mad at me. Why do I always have to listen to conversations that are not meant for me, why can't I just be like Willy and mind my own business?

Yes, why? I ask myself. Now I am grounded, no phone for me this week.

SEPTEMBER 21ST

I HATE P.E. I HATE P.E. I HATE P.E. I HATE P.E.

The teacher makes us run around the basketball court eight times, jump between tires, run with one leg tied to another person's leg—I'm always paired with Susana who's SO SLOW and is really pigeon-toed.

Tere says I have to be patient with Susana because of her mom. But so what, I know that she doesn't have a mom, but she is pigeon-toed and doesn't run good. Tere says, Winning isn't everything. She also says I can be very mean sometimes.

Pinche Tere.

I can't help it if Susana falls. She stays sitting on the bench and cleans her scrapes with a towel the teacher gives her.

The teacher then pairs me up with Mercedes. Mercedes can run good and she doesn't cry for anything.

When classes are over, Mercedes and I exchange phone numbers.

SEPTEMBER 23RD

Tere is upset because I asked Mercedes to hang out with us. Tere doesn't understand that the more, the merrier. She doesn't like Mercedes, she says that Mercedes feels that she is better than us.

Mercedes *is* better than us, her dad lives in the States and sends her and her mother and brothers money, lots of money.

I try hard to convince her that Mercedes is cool. She says, Whatever.

SEPTEMBER 25TH

Every other day we either hear shootings or hear about shootings all over town. That is normal.

But just the other day, something else happened! There was a massive shootout downtown. We never go downtown anymore, but now downtown is definitely out of the question. One of our neighbors was driving around the area and got hurt. I heard Mamá say that his lung was compromised. I don't know what that means, but I bet it's bad news.

Bad news, we live in a town that is all bad news.

SEPTEMBER 28TH

Mamá didn't take us to school again. She said her gut told her not to. Too dangerous to go out today.

Well, tell your gut to explain that to the principal of my school, I said. We've been skipping school way too much. You are right, she said, if only you two could be homeschooled.

What does that mean? I ask her.

She says that it is just like it sounds—it's like school, but at home. I would be in charge of teaching you and Willy every day. It is a very common practice in the States.

I told her I didn't wanna practice that, no way. I don't like school, no one does, but school is the only place where I can actually talk to people and have fun.

Well, today that is what we are going to do, have fun, she said, and she gave us things to color in her studio.

The hours flew by. It wasn't all that bad after all. But still, I am hoping tomorrow she takes us back to school.

SEPTEMBER 30TH

Once again I hear Mamá tell Tía on the phone that she is gonna try to convince Papá to move to El Paso. I don't know what to do, she says, things are getting really heavy around here. I am always afraid the phone is gonna ring with bad news, she says.

When she is done talking to Tía, I tell her about Mercedes' dad. How he lives in the States and how he will soon bring Mercedes and her mom with him to live up north. He has a different name up there, I tell her.

I see Mamá looking at me, like she doesn't understand me, and I explain to her what Mercedes told me, that her dad is using someone else's identity to have a social security number to be able to work legally. Mamá tells me that what Mercedes' dad is doing is not legal, but it is what everyone else does anyway.

So, why can't Papá do something like that? Why can't we just leave this place once and for all?

We can't, Mamá says, it is not that easy.

But you want us to go, that's exactly what you told Tía, that you wanted us all to go and…

Stop it, Julia, she says. Just stop it.

OCTOBER 3RD

Dear Diary:

You are probably the only one who loves me in this
house. Mamá hates me. Papá hates me. Willy, he
doesn't hate me maybe, but one day he will.

But the one who hates me the most is Mamá. She
really hates my guts. You see, Papá came back and as
always he brought us gifts and money, and I said, Thank
you, thank you, thank you, Papá. Then he sat down to
watch TV, Willy took his boots off, Mamá opened a beer
for him, I looked at the whole scene as if it was a movie.
I thought, Will we still get gifts and money if we move to
El Paso?

I asked him and he said, We are not moving to El Paso,
where did you get that idea? I told him I heard Mamá with
Tía and then they started arguing, the yelling, you should
have heard all the yelling. Mamá told him that moving to El
Paso was something I imagined.

But it wasn't, you know it.

Later that night Mamá said to promise not to lie
anymore.

I wasn't lying, you know it.

I said it, I am not lying, you know I am not, you know you want to, you know you want to live in El Paso because you are afraid of living… I didn't even get to finish my sentence. Mamá slapped me and told me to shut the fuck up.

I know that if I told anyone about this no one would believe
me: Willy is Papá's favorite. See, when Papá comes back from
work (which can be at 1:00 pm, at 9:00 pm, or two days after
that), he always goes and kisses Willy on the forehead. He
comes to my room sometimes, but he only whispers, Nite nite,
little girl.

I hate to be called *little girl* or *girl*. Why can't they get that I
am already thirteen?

I wonder, if Willy is Papá's favorite, am I Mamá's?

Papá takes Willy to watch soccer at a friend's house every
Sunday. Therefore, every Sunday is Girl's Day. That's what
Mamá calls it. We eat a sweet-sugar-sugary breakfast. We
watch TV and do each other's nails. I love it. It's like I am then
her Favorite. Sunday is the only day Mamá doesn't lock herself
up in her studio. She just draws on her notepad, but right next
to me. It's just us girls hanging out.

Today we watch a chick-flick. The movie is about a man
named Benjamin who is grumpy and mean to everybody,
especially with a woman called Andie, so she tries to teach him
a lesson. I liked Andie, I thought that was a guy's name. I guess
you can name your kids however you want. Anyway, Benjamin
and Andie end up falling in love with each other even though
there are things they don't like about each other. I thought that
was cute. I guess you can love someone even when you don't
like him that much.

At some point I looked at Mamá and said, You've never told

me how you met Papá. Mamá stayed there, quiet, thinking, thinking. How come adults take SOOO long to answer the simplest questions? Finally she said, I have known him my whole life.

I asked, What do you mean? Since you were kids?

She smiled, Sort of, yes.

I am fascinated now. I pause the movie and ask her, Wait, were you in love since you were kids? And then? Did you wait to grow up to get married?

Mamá smiled and said, I don't know if we really grew up.

I didn't understand her. I told her so: Mamá, I don't understand. But she hits play and the movie is back on. She is not watching the movie anymore. Her attention is on her notebook and her dark charcoal drawing. Is that a heart? I asked her, but she did not reply.

Bis says that all women have only one big love. Papá is Mamá's big love. Papá is her favorite, not Willy nor me. Papá.

OCTOBER 13TH

Yesterday we did not have classes, and today we had a guest. It was this lady who came to teach us how to take care of ourselves. How to be careful. She gave us a list of DO NOT'S.

- Do not talk to strangers.
- Do not accept anything from anyone you don't know.
- Do not answer the phone if you are alone at home.
- Do not go out if you hear shooting or yelling.
- Do not go out late in the afternoon or at night, not even to the corner store.

The list was way longer. She also said that in this city almost 1,500 people have died just this year.

That's a whole bunch of dead people, one kid said. We all laughed. The lady told us it was no laughing matter.

I guess it is **NOT** a laughing matter.

She also told us that we lived in a very dangerous city and in very dangerous times. She told us the State and the narcos are taking everything from us. What do you exactly mean by **EVERYTHING**, I wanted to ask, but didn't.

Then Mercedes whispered to me. Julia, Julia, look at the lady's blouse, it is a bit see-through. She was right, you could see her bra through the fabric. It was kinda funny, and I was about to share that with Tere, but when I looked at her she had big fat tears on her cheeks. Tere, I whispered, what's wrong?

She's crying because of her dad, Miguel told me.

Because of her dad?

That's right.

Kids in school are starting to say that Tere's dad was involved with bad people, the narcos. But she always says what everybody says when you have a relative who's disappeared, is dead or in jail: *He was not involved with the narcos or anything like that, he was just in the wrong place at the wrong time.*

It seems that too many people HERE have been in the wrong place at the wrong time. Hundreds and hundreds.

OCTOBER 18TH

Yesterday Willy and I had to go with Mamá to a café with her friends. There was no one to babysit us. Her friend turned on the TV for us. But she wouldn't let us watch the soap opera even though we told them we *are* allowed to watch it. We had to watch stupid cartoons.

I was going to use the bathroom when I heard Mamá and her friends talking about some girls.

They went missing like a month ago. They were cousins. They went everywhere together. They were in the same school. They always walked back home together.

They say one day they just did not show up after class. It was the talk everywhere, how could you not know?

Well, they finally found them. They were on a wasteland.

Yes, they were obviously raped, hurt, and then killed. That's what "they" do. That's all they do.

Everyone always talks about *they*. Who is THEY anyway?

Mamá and her friends wonder how the mothers of those girls will survive this. They wonder how *someone* can do something like this. How can *someone* be so soulless?

Soulless, that's a new word.

I go back to watching TV with Willy. I repeat the word soulless to myself. I wonder what it means. I wonder what rape means. I wonder what all this means. Is this what that lady at school was talking about?

Then I remember what the kids in school told me once, there are matañiñitas in town.

OCTOBER 18TH, 8 PM

soulless.

(of a building, room, or other place)

- lacking character and individuality
- having no soul or no greatness or warmth of mind or feeling
- tedious and uninspiring
- lacking or suggesting the lack of human feelings and qualities, e.g., "two soulless black eyes were watching her"

OCTOBER 26TH

Our neighbors disappeared. Just like that, from one day to another. Gone. That happens a lot here: people leave, they move back to wherever they are from or to wherever is not the state of Chihuahua. Some lucky ones go to El Paso. But when somebody leaves there are parties and goodbyes. Not these neighbors.

They did not even say goodbye. It's not that we were close to them, aside from the fact that, **HELLO**, we were their neighbors. But still, nothing, they said nothing. They were on their own all the time. They did not talk to any of us on our street. Well, the mom did say good morning to Mamá. The dad and Papá would do that thing men do, nod with half a smile whenever they saw each other.

They had twins, two girls, almost as old as Willy. They had a cat. Those girls were always trying to pretend the cat was their baby. His name is Califas. I remember I asked them one day why did they give their cat that name. They said, Dunno. I would never give the name Califas to anyone.

I was the one who noticed that the neighbors had gone. I heard Califas from our backyard. He was crying and crying. I went in and told Mamá, Don't you hear? Califas is crying. He's been crying a lot. Do you think something happened to him? You know, like it happened to Marta's dog or like it happened to…

Mamá hates when I talk about all the pets that have been killed or run over in our neighborhood. Without taking her eyes from her painting she said, That's-not-our-business.

I can't help it. I like things that are not-our-business.

Then I did what I sometimes do when Mamá ignores me. I called Papá. I called him on his cell (yeah, he now has a cell!) and told him: Papá, Califas is crying and crying. I think something bad has happened.

Papá said, Who the fuck is Califas? He sounded mad.

The cat, Papá, the neighbor's cat, I said.

And what the fuck do you want me to do? I have told you not to call me for stupid little things, Julia.

Papá sounds more and more mad lately. He is using the F-word way too much. Sometimes I can't help it and start crying when he talks like that. Not this time, I didn't care what he said, I told him: Califas is crying, and he never cries this much, I am sure something happened, you always tell us to be aware of what happens around us, and I tell you, something has happened next door. Should I go check?

No, don't do anything. Stay there, but be alert. I am on my way.

I felt like a detective from *Law & Order*, yeah, the one I am not supposed to watch, Papá's favorite show. I stayed alert right next to the door until Papá arrived. I saw him getting out of his car, walking to our neighbor's house. I couldn't help it, I opened the front door and joined him.

The house was empty. We could see the emptiness from the windows. There was nothing, no curtains, no furniture, no pictures hanging from the walls, there wasn't even a welcome mat. Nothing, they left nothing but silence. Well, silence and a crying cat.

Papá called someone on his phone. I hear him say, Sánchez is gone.

I walked around the house. Their backyard door was open. I opened it. I saw Califas. He saw me, but instead of running away, he walked toward me.

I don't understand it, how can someone leave and forget a cat? Especially a cat that cries like Califas does. Meow, meow, they left me, is probably what Califas was trying to say. Meow, meow, they forgot about me.

Papá came to the neighbor's backyard. He found me caressing Califas. Can I keep him? I asked.

We'll see.

Pedro arrived a bit later. Pedro is Papá's friend and partner. They are always together lately. By then Mamá and Willy were also outside.

What's going on? Mamá asked.

I gave her a full report and told her, Papá says we might keep the cat.

Papá denied it, but by then Califas was already in Willy's hands who was saying, Yes, let's keep it, let's keep the cat.

OCTOBER 28TH

Ladies and Gentlemen!
It is official: Willy and I now have a CAT!

OCTOBER 30TH

Mercedes and I like playing questions and answers. Today we did questions and answers about her grandma and my bis.

Mercedes: Yours drinks tea? Mine drinks whiskey.

Me: Does she like knitting?

Mercedes: I told you, she likes whiskey.

Me: Mmhh.

Mercedes: Mine reads and re-reads her old cowboy-romance novels.

Me: Mine watches soap operas.

Mercedes: Does your bis have a husband?

Me: That's a good question. She had two. How about yours?

Mercedes: Not anymore, but she has a lot of boyfriends.

Me: Wow.

Mercedes: Mine is talking on the phone all the time.

Me: Mine talks to herself.

NOVEMBER 18TH

Papá finally got a visa. He says that he was almost certain he wouldn't get it, but he did. I am so glad he did because now we can cross all together.

Papá is happy, he says we're going to get the new car and that we're going shopping and that we're going to eat juicy ribs at a nice place. Mamá is not happy.

But it is what you wanted, I told her.

Not this way, she said, now we owe *them*.

Them?

I guess Mamá realized she said something she shouldn't have because when I ask her again who them is, she says, Forget it. Let's concentrate on the good news. Now all of us get to go to your tía's.

Well, I say, we could go this weekend, we don't have classes on Friday because of Revolution Day and...

No, no, Mamá says, too soon. She insists we need to plan. Perhaps for Christmas she says.

Why do adults make everything so difficult?

NOVEMBER 26TH

Mercedes got her period last weekend. Before her it was Natalia, and before Natalia, it was Susana, before Susana it was Tere, and before Tere pretty much every girl in my class got it. Or maybe not, but it feels that I am the only one who hasn't gotten it. Our biology teacher says everyone's body is different.

I hate my body for being different and for being late. I am late to everything in life. Mercedes says that long ago, before she got her period, her mother promised her that she would be allowed to shave her legs once she became a woman

A woman? I asked.

Yes, that's what you become once you get your period, she said.

So, this is my life, I am either the new-girl-in-school or the-only-girl-in school-who-hasn't-gotten-her-period. PERIOD!

DECEMBER 18TH

Today we are going to El Paso. We are spending Christmas there. Mamá suggested that we go a few days early to avoid all the craziness.

What craziness? Willy asked. The craziness of the long line at the bridge, she said. But she was wrong, the craziness is already here. We've been waiting for hours now, so here I am writing and writing while we wait.

I am so nervous that I don't feel butterflies in my stomach, they are more like huge fat pigeons. My hands are sweating. Papá and Mamá have told us like a hundred times that if we are asked we have to say, No sir, we do not have relatives in the U.S. Papá asks me to practice it a couple of times in English, because I am the only one who actually speaks English. He wants me to say, *In the United States*, instead of, *In the U.S.*, but I told him no one says *United States* anymore.

Mamá tells him it might be a bit suspicious if I speak English and they don't. Papá says, I want them to see that we are not as stupid as they think.

Mamá tells him no one cares, but Papá insists. OK, OK, she says, always giving in to Papá's wishes.

When we are getting close, Papá gets out of the car and says, See you guys on the other side.

He kisses Mamá and waves good-bye to us.

Why is he leaving? Willy asks.

Because he wasn't born there, like us, and it would be a bit suspicious and…

I don't understand what she says. Why does everything have to be so weird in our family?

The line is L o o o o o o o N G. Cars and cars and cars and cars. Some people are selling stuff. Some people, people like us, just sit still inside their cars, waiting and waiting. Willy says, Wake me up when we get there. And he curls up like Califas when he is tired.

As we get closer to the checkpoint, the vendors start to disappear. It is only us now, the ones in the cars, us and some officers who walk around the lines with humongous dogs. I remember Tere telling me about them, the dogs, the police dogs, the spy dogs. These dogs, they get anything, they know if you are carrying drugs. I looked at her and she added, Yes, Julia, there are people whose work it is to take drugs to the U.S. Don't tell me you didn't know about this? I pretended that I did, that I did know that and much more.

Is it true that some people just cross the border to bring drugs? I ask Mamá.

She looks at me, then looks at the bridge, then at me again and says, Who told you about this? Don't tell me. Your tía? Your bis?

I tell her I heard about it in school.

What they teach kids these days, she says before turning the radio on.

I pay attention to the line again, I see the dogs passing by, smelling everything. They are too big, they are too obvious to be spies. Why don't they use cats, I wonder. They should use cats, cats are smarter, and they can squeeze into anything. Plus they are better actors, they purr at you, they smile at you, and you think, Oh, this cat likes me! and then they get you with their claws when you least expect it. Yeah, cats would be better than dogs.

Mamá says, Practice one last time what Papá told you to say, it is almost our turn.

But you said…

Come on, Julia, just do it.

We are just going shopping. I am gonna buy a hundred pairs of shoes, I tell the officer who asks me what I'm going to do in El Paso.

A hundred?

I have probably made it sound suspicious. I correct myself. OK, only one.

He laughs first, then he asks Mamá how come we live in México. Mamá tells him that it's cheaper.

Way cheaper, he says and smiles. He checks out Willy who is kinda awake and kinda not.

We did it, we crossed the border, we did it, we finally did it. We are going to see the rest of the family. We'll go to Tía's house, we will see Bis and Jonás, my cousin who I haven't seen in ages. I hate that our whole family is divided by a border and a bridge.

DECEMBER 18TH, STILL WAITING IN LINE

Things people sell on the bridge:

- candies
- popsicles
- chicharrones with salsa
- candles with the face of the virgin, Jesus, and many other guys.
- balloons
- necklaces made of beans
- piggy banks
- key chains
- bottles of water
- cans of soda
- candies
- candies

TWO

"Ever notice happy kids don't write
in their diaries very much? They don't have to.
Life's too fun. Diaries are for when life isn't fun.
They are for figuring what went wrong."

Lesley Arfin, *Dear Diary*

DECEMBER 22ND

We are having the most wonderfulest time ever. We go shopping almost every day. At first, it was great to see all the decorations and the Christmas spirit everywhere, but now the carols drive us crazy. *We wish you a merry Christmas, we wish you a merry Christmas, we wish…* Ay, it gives me a headache just to think about it.

But other than that, we are having fun. I hang out with Jonás all the time. He is cool and not weird about talking to girls like the boys at my school. He plays with Willy, the three of us watch movies til midnight.

Jonás doesn't have a dad. Well, he does, but he is just nowhere to be found when you need him the most, Jonás says. Papá travels a lot too, I tell him. But Jonás says it is not the same, his dad just disappears, and then he comes back banging doors, drunk and yelling. We don't like him, he says. Our moms know how to choose them, he adds. I don't know what he means and whatever.

Jonás is teaching me to ride his bike. I had never been on one before. I fell off only like a thousand times before I finally got the hang of it. And you know what? In El Paso, kids can actually ride bikes everywhere. Jonás comes and goes to the corner store or to the bakery all alone on his bike. That would never happen in Juárez. Never ever.

I wish I had learned to bike before writing my Christmas letter. I could have asked Santa for a bike. Now I will be stuck with shoes, clothes, and, if I'm lucky, an iPod. But maybe I'll get lucky and "Santa" will realize what I really need and want is a bike. Now I can only think about having a bright pink bike. A bike to fly.

Ok, I am not stupid, I know bikes cannot fly, but that's how it feels to ride a bike, it feels like you are flying off, flying away from your family, your city, your problems, flying off from everything and being free free free.

Papá says that if "Santa" does not bring me a bike, I can always ask the Three Wise Men for one, I tell Jonás, and when I get it, I will name her Vicky.

Jonás says, Bikes are not like dolls. You don't give them names, you just call them bikes and ride them.

I yell back at him and tell him that I can do whatever I want with the bike I will get soon. Mamá hears us and says, No, young lady, forget about a bike, you can't have a bike at home.

I ask her, Why why why can't I?

It's just too dangerous, she says.

I cry and cry and cry and cry. Even Jonás who thinks I am stupid for wanting to name a bike I will never have comes and hugs me. He says I can use his bike every time I come and visit. But I can't help it, I cry and cry and cry because I hate that I never get what I want, like to play on the street and own a bike.

Bis comes and hugs me. Come on, pumpkin pie, don't cry, don't cry. Let's just write that letter to the Three Wise Men and tell them to bring your bike here to us. Jonás adds, Yes, let's do that. I can take care of your Vicky when you are not here. Now stop crying and let's go out.

DECEMBER 25TH

Well, it happened. I got everything I asked for, EXCEPT a bike.

At least Christmas was fun and it snowed. From the window we can still see that everything is white, even the mountain with the star. White, everything white.

Tía, can we play in the snow?

Yes, you can, but make sure you are all warm, she says.

Jonás, Willy and I put on thermals, thick socks, sweaters, jackets, beanies, and gloves to go out and play on the white streets of El Paso. Some other kids from the block join us. All of us walk to a park on the street called Montana. Like Hanna Montana, I say.

Montana is the longest street on the planet, Jonás says.

On the planet? Willy asks.

OK, maybe not on the planet, maybe just the longest in El Paso.

Montana, I kinda like how it sounds.

We have snowball battles and draw snow angels with our bodies and try to do a snowman, but it looks more like a planet snow. We are all having so much fun. I like playing with everybody, but I especially like just hanging out with Jonás. He speaks Spanish as if he had just chewed a lot of ice. From time to time, he forgets how to say things, so he just says it in English. He tells me all about his school. Wiggs Middle School, he says.

Wiggs. I really like how it sounds.

I wish you guys lived here, like us, Jonás says. We could go to school together, we could play, we could bike all summer long. Would you want to?

Live here? I say. I don't know.

Even though I know I want to.

Papá doesn't want to, I say, but I do, really bad, but I just need to want something very bad for Mamá and Papá to say no.

Yeah, it's the same with my mom, Jonás says.

Living here would be great, I would get to be with Bis and speak English all the time, and I could play on the streets AND AND AND…

Will I forget my Spanish just like you? I ask Jonás.

I haven't forgotten my Spanish, you dummy.

But he has, I can tell when he does, I can tell when he is trying to say something and digs deep in his brain to find a word.

I like it though. I like how everything is here: half Spanish, half English, half old, half new.

H
   A
      L
        F.

DECEMBER 28TH

Vacation is almost over, and I still haven't gotten my period. I am still a kid, a pinche kid, a fucking kid and I hate it. That's what I tell Jonás: I hate being a kid, I wanna get my period.

He says, Wooo, too much information. He blushes and says, I don't wanna know about that kind of girl stuff.

Me neither, I say, because I don't wanna be a girl, I wanna be a woman, I am thirteen now, and I wanna be a woman like all my friends.

I can make you a woman, he says, if you let me.

APRIL 17TH

I haven't written in months. Mamá was concerned about me and my not writing because she knows I normally do it all the time. She offered to buy me a new diary. She even said, Don't tell me you don't like writing anymore. I told her I still liked it, of course, I will be a writer one day, but I just didn't feel like it.

It's just that after vacation, things got weird.

Let's call it Boy drama and Family drama.

The only good thing that has happened in this world is that the old lady killer was finally caught, and oh yes, Papá is making more money, but still I don't see a pink bike in my future.

Mamá sees me writing. She smiles. She says, Us artists need to keep on working. Working makes us happy. I tell her that I don't know if I'm happy, I just know that I am ready to write again. She asks, Will you write about our Christmas vacation? About your aunt's house? About your games on the snow? About Jonás?

The last thing I wanna write about is Jonás. I hate him now. If I could, I would erase him from our family trip, erase him forever.

APRIL 19TH

Fine, I will write about Jonás and what happened.

He promised to make me a woman. I didn't believe him, but he said he could, he said he had that power, he said all men had the power of turning little girls into young women.

But you really need to do what I say, or else it won't work.

I did what he said: I stood there, I closed my eyes, and then he kissed me. And I hated it, I hated him.

APRIL 24TH

I love Saturdays because Pedro always comes to our house, but now it will be even better because Pedro will be staying with us for a while. This time Papá will take a very long trip, and Mamá is freaking out. She says we can't be left alone, what if something happens and…long story short, Pedro is staying.

I like Pedro a lot, Willy too. Mamá, not that much.

Pedro is Papá's oldest friend, and now he is an *associate*, as Papá says. Pedro and Papá have known each other since like forever. Sometimes weeks, months and entire seasons go by without seeing Pedro. Then, when we least expect it, he comes home.

Papá says that Pedro is like those dogs that aren't yours but still come back for you to pet them. I don't think it is nice to say that a person is a dog. But, if Pedro is a dog, he is a Rottweiler on the outside, but a bunny on the inside. He has a soft heart.

I wonder where Pedro goes when he is not around.

Now that he started working with Papá, we see him almost every day, unless they are away. You see, if Papá travels, Pedro travels with him. When Papá gets in his handy-man mood, Pedro gets in it too. Like a shadow.

Yeah, Pedro is like Papá's new shadow.

I learn a lot with Pedro, the other day he taught me to do long hand-shakes with gestures and everything. I like it when he tells old stories, like those from the time he played baseball. I also like it when he tells me about the ranch he was born on.

APRIL 28TH

Willy says I have a crush on Pedro. Where did he get that idea?
I like him, I can't deny it. It is just so easy to talk to him, to hang
out with him. He answers all my questions. Or most of them.

Mamá keeps telling him he needs a sweetheart.

I asked him once, Why don't you have a family, Pedro?

He smiled and said, Because I have you all, duh!

We laugh.

Then Willy added, No, a family of your own, like your own
wife, your own kids, your own cat?

Pedro caressed Willy's head and told him that he didn't
need any other family but us.

Pedro has tattoos all over. Pedro has lots of scars. And
stories, he's got so many of them. Like the one when they—
Papá and him and some other kids—stole bread from the
bakery and then they ran fast, so fast that no one caught
them. Or that story of the boy who took his dad's gun and
shot himself while playing with it. Guns are not toys, I tell you,
Pedro said. Don't forget it.

MAY 4TH

Tere tells Mercedes and me that once classes are over in June she will leave. She is going to live elsewhere.

Are you moving across the bridge? I ask her because that is what everyone does when they leave this place.

No, we are not.

Are you going far? Mercedes asks.

Tere nods.

Is your brother also leaving? I ask, but it is a stupid question because her whole family is leaving obviously. I wanna ask her about her dad, is he free now and that is why they are moving or are they leaving him behind to rot in jail?

I am kinda sad that she is leaving, but to tell you the truth, we weren't hanging out as much as we used to. I haven't written about it here, but a few weeks ago we got into a huge fight because she says that I am not thankful for what the Lord gives me. She says I am too full of myself. Like that day when you brought that huge cake for the party and you made everyone else prefer yours better than Pepe's, who made such an effort to bring his. I don't know where she got that from: his cake wasn't big or heavy, and his mom made it, so what effort?

She also said that everything comes too easy for girls like me.

Girls like me? I asked her.

Yes, girls like you, with fathers like yours.

What's wrong with my father? I said.

Don't pretend you don't know, it is obvious he is doing

something he is not supposed to because all of a sudden you guys have a car and a house and…

I couldn't take it. Well, at least, my father is not in jail, like yours, I said. And just as I was saying it, I sorta regretted it.

Who told you THAT? she asked.

I could have said that it was Mamá who told me, so I could always be good and sweet with poor Tere, but instead I said, Everyone in school knows THAT.

She looked at me, I could see her brain cooking the best words to get back at me. Well, EVERYONE knows that your dad is washing money for the narcos, and he will be caught one day and he will end up worse than my dad, way worse.

I pushed her away and left. I heard her calling me, *Julia, Julia.* But I ignored her. Stupid Tere.

Anyway, after the fight, we didn't talk for weeks. Until now. She was the one who started talking to me. Out of the blue. She told me about moving away and then she said, I am sorry, Julia.

I looked at her and said, I am sorry too. But I am not sure I am sorry. She did invent stuff about Papá after all.

I wanna ask Mamá about washing money for narcos, like, how do you do that, but it feels like a bad idea.

MAY 7TH

Bis will stay here for a few days. She likes Pedro because he keeps telling her that no one in the world makes green chile burritos like she does. The truth is that lately her green chile burritos are not all that green. She isn't herself. Her mind is somewhere else.

For example, she was explaining to me a couple of things from the Magician of her tarot deck. She kept looking at the card but didn't say anything, went blank. She went, What was I telling you?

Then all of a sudden she will go and say, I want ice cream. I want a strawberry ice cream. Come on, let's go, let's all go get ice cream. Ice cream. **ICE CREAM!** She says it and I picture her as a little girl. A little girl who wants ice cream. She and Willy look exactly the same age, he is just as happy as she is.

Today she got that ice cream craziness and we went to get it. Pedro took us. I had a shake, a delicious shake. Mamá didn't get anything, she was with us, but she wasn't with us. Her mind was probably in the drawing. Or her mind is with Papá. Sometimes I think that Papá and art are the only things in Mamá's mind.

MAY 8TH

So Pedro doesn't have a family for reals. He doesn't have a mom or a dad. Just like Mamá, he was raised by his grandma and with a tía, Tía María. They live in Parral. Pedro sends them money, buys them things like microwaves or fridges or fans with an ice tray to keep them cold. My grandma is losing her sight, Pedro says, but she is too stubborn and won't have a surgery. I tell him that Bis is not losing her sight, but that she loses everything else all the time and doesn't wanna go to the doctor.

She is a stubborn one, right? he says.

I look at Pedro and share my wisdom with him. All women are very stubborn, Pedro, you should know it by now.

Pedro laughs. He always laughs at what I say. Where did you get that from? he asks.

I tell him that I have heard Papá say so. He says that when he and Mamá are arguing. He says all women are too stubborn, stubborn like mules.

Is that true? I ask him.

Possibly maybe, Pedro says.

It must be really difficult not to see, I say. I close my eyes just enough to see a bit of light through my eyelashes. I walk around the living room, the kitchen.

Careful, Pedro says.

Have you ever considered getting married? I ask him while I walk around the living room.

Where did that come from? he asks me.

I dunno, you are Papá's age and you don't have a wife, you don't have kids, you just have your grannie and your tía.

After thinking and thinking for a while he says, Not everyone has to get married and have kids.

But what if…what if you fall crazy in love?

Pedro looks at the ceiling, like he's looking for an answer. The ceiling must have made him tell me, You don't have to get married when you fall in love…you just…you just have to love, that's it. The rest is bullshit.

I kinda wanted to tell him that I loved him very, very much. I wanted to tell him that I have dreamt I am older and he wants to marry me because he loves me. But I know he is gonna tell me that's bullshit and that I am way too young to be talking about love.

I hate it when people say that. I am almost fourteen, after all!

I sometimes daydream he is my husband, and he is like Papá. He gives me kisses on my cheeks, my forehead, my lips, my neck. I dream that he pulls my hair, I dream that he slams doors when he is angry, calls me stubborn and then kisses me again. I dream that he goes away on trips and that I wait for him.

Just like Mamá waits for Papá.

MAY 14TH

Mercedes says Pepe likes me.

Of course he likes me, I said, I make him laugh all the time.

No, idiot, she says, even though I've told her a million times that I hate her calling me an idiot. Pepe likes you likes you, like he is in love with you. What do you want me to tell him? she asks.

Tell him? I say.

Yes, you gotta tell me what you want me to say to him, you know, about him liking you.

But why? I ask.

Mercedes says this is the way it works with boys and girls:

- a boy likes a girl
- the girl is told that boy likes her
- the boy expects a message
- a relationship starts or not

I tell Mercedes the truth. I tell her I don't like Pepe. I try to make it clear that I like him, but I don't like him like him. Mercedes says I am lucky to be liked by Pepe. Then, stupid me, I go and say, You know? I actually like René, I like him like him because…and when I try to explain to her why I like René, she says I can't like him because she likes him and she gets super mad and says we can't be friends anymore.

I don't understand a thing. It's like the older you get, the more complicated things are.

MAY 15TH

I told Pedro about this whole thing with Mercedes and Pepe and René and me. Pedro told me the other day that everything starts with a kiss. Wars, stories, everything. I ask him about his first kiss, and he says that it sucked. I laugh. Then he said that he would break the arm of the first stupid kid that tries to kiss me, because I am his princess, and no one kisses his princess.

Not even you? I asked him.

Especially not me, he said.

This Sunday we will take Bis back home. That means that I will see Jonás. I don't know what we will say to each other. I am not mad at him anymore for what happened last December. I don't want to erase him from the face of the earth, as I had planned. Now I just want him to do it again, to kiss me. I want him to say that practice kisses between cousins are OK.

MAY 17TH

Today some people came to our class to talk to us about elections. They gave us a brochure. I was about to turn mine into a fan when the teacher said that we are to underline the words we didn't understand and then ask our guests what those words mean.

> The Politics of Mexico take place in a framework of a federal presidential representative <u>democratic</u> republic whose government is based on a...**BLAH BLAH BLAH**...

Pepe raised his hand before anyone, like always. He asked how come Mexico is called the United Mexican States, it sounds like the United States, are we like the United States? The teacher didn't even let our guests answer his question. She reminded Pepe, and all of us, that we had already discussed that in class. Then René asked what did the word democratic exactly mean. I had also underlined that word. Sounds like a pill, doesn't it? One of the guests, the guy with the tie, explained what democracy meant. He also said that religion should not be part of our education. I wonder if they know that at our school on Mondays they make us sing about how much the lord loves us.

Later on I raised my hand and asked what were the differences between executive, legislative and federal. I just did it to make my teacher proud. She likes it when we ask our guests questions.

Tere was the last one to raise her hand, but instead of asking something she stood up and told everyone that her mother thought the Mexican constitution was bullshit, a lie, something that was invented to keep us quiet. She also said that her mother did not believe in democracy and that Calderón and the federales are just like the inquisition, and, because none of us could understand, she then said, Imagine our President Calderón is like Voldemort and the federales like the dementors of Harry Potter.

No shit.

Tere was getting herself in trouble when the bell rang and we all went out to recess.

Tere, what did you mean back there? Pepe asked her.

Tere said that she was no fool, and we should not be fooled either. She said that if her dad was in prison, it was because of our so-called democracy, because we are all in the hands of a system that needs guinea pigs.

Guinea pigs? I asked.

Yes, guinea pigs: people who are only used and abused by the system. People who are falsely blamed for someone else's mistakes. She then told us that the system invented that her dad shot someone else. Number one, he never had a gun. Number two, he didn't even know the person who he supposedly shot. I tell you, the system is all bullshit.

Tere kept saying things, but in the back of my mind I could only think about the word bullshit and, also, about the fact that when Tere talks, it is actually her mom talking. At least that is what Mamá said when I told her about this.

MAY 19TH

Today we almost had a fire. Well, more like Bis almost started a fire. She was visiting for the weekend and told us she would make fried chicken, but then she started singing and dancing all over the house, some song that I had never heard, a song about perfume and women. It was so funny, I mean it was funny until we all realized that something smelled like burning. The kitchen was taken by a white mist. It's burning, it's burning, Willy and I yelled. But it was like she didn't get it.

Until she did. Oh my god, the chicken! she said.

It was scary, I won't lie. Sometimes, when she does things like this and no one else is around, I feel like I'm the adult and have to take care of the situation.

The chicken looked like charcoal and tasted like ashes, so we didn't eat it. But I ordered pizza with the allowance Papá gives me, so that's what we ended up eating. Who doesn't love pizza?

When Mamá got home, the first thing she said was, It smells weird here. We did not say anything, there was no need. She found out by herself: a black pan and a piece of charcoal chicken was all she needed to see to understand.

Mamá preached at Bis like she was a little girl. She reminded her that yesterday she gave us toasted fajitas, and the day before it was the tortillas, and now the chicken? It's like Mamá takes note of all of Bis' mistakes. Bis doesn't mind though, she only smiles and says, We ordered pizza, come on, have a slice.

MAY 22ND

Mercedes will come home for a sleepover, and I am $oooo
excited! This is my first sleepover ever.

We are gonna watch movies, and we are gonna do each
other's nails and hair and then we are gonna lock ourselves in
my room and talk about the boys from school and stay up late
telling horror stories or sexy stories or whatever stories.

MAY 23RD

The sleepover wasn't as much fun as I thought, and now
Mercedes and I aren't talking to each other. We had a fight, a
stupid fight, but I guess I understood how she really is.

Details later.

Or never.

MAY 24TH

When I was a kid I liked Hannah Montana because she was like two girls at once. One was a regular girl, a girl who went to school, did homework, had a friend, and all that.

The other one was not your everyday girl because she was famous and a singer and everybody loved her, cheered her, and also everyone wanted to be like her, like Hannah Montana. Hell, I wanted to be like Hannah Montana!

I don't know when I stopped watching Hannah Montana. But today, I saw Willy watching a 24-hour Hannah Montana marathon on Tía's TV, and it got me thinking.

I think I also liked Hannah Montana because of her dad. I loved how he always took care of her, took her everywhere, and helped her out of any mess. Papá would be caught dead before helping me out of any mess, like the other day when me and Mercedes got in trouble for skipping class and Mamá slapped me. He did nothing, he just watched the whole thing happen. Hannah Montana's dad would have never let that happen.

Mine? Mine just said, I am gonna be away again, you better not worry your mom or else...

MAY 28TH

My P.E. teacher was killed. We were told what we are always told when someone is killed. She died. Just that, she died. There was no other explanation, no one told us things like, She was sick, she had an accident, or she was killed, no. She died, she just did, don't ask any questions, period.

There's a big black ribbon on our school's gate. If you think about it, there are way too many of those ribbons all over the city. I wonder who makes them? That's some business.

When I saw that ribbon, I thought of the first time I saw one. It was in the corner store of the neighborhood where we used to live. The son of the corner store lady died. He just died, that's what everyone said. But the lady told the truth to anyone willing to hear. My son was killed, he was killed, those people killed him. They killed him just because he was in the wrong place at the wrong time.

A black ribbon means mourning. It means we are mourning someone we love.

I wonder if someone in Miss Fernandez' family—instead of just saying she died—says, She was killed, my daughter was killed, she was killed for being in the wrong place at the wrong time.

JUNE 1ST

Classes are almost over, summer is coming.

    The good thing about the summer: we go to El Paso.

    The bad thing about the summer: it is hot.

    The really bad thing about the summer: Tere is moving.

JUNE 5TH

Papá is back.

But it is like he left and someone else's dad came back. He is different. Skinnier. Grumpier. He sleeps all day long. He doesn't talk, he whispers. He whispers with Mamá. He only nods yes or no to us. He smokes, he smokes a lot.

He gets mad at every little thing. He doesn't watch that TV show that he used to like, he only watches soccer games or food shows.

Mamá is the only one allowed to be close to him. She kisses him, she hugs him, but at the same time she lets him be. She doesn't ask him anything, that's what he made us promise: no questions about his work, his trips, no questions at all.

We can't make noise at home. We can't play music, we can't play good against bad, we can't shoot each other when we play because Papá needs silence. That's what Mamá says.

It's like Papá is Mamá's son.

JUNE 6TH

Mamá is in a very good mood. When she is in a very good mood, she sings. Mamá is singing. I have never heard that song, but it is a love song.

She takes some coffee to Papá, drinks hers next to him. They stay in bed longer than usual. What's really incredible is that she doesn't say anything to us even though we are already watching cartoons and eating choco-krispies. Willy stands up and goes with them to bed. They all laugh. Willy calls me. *Julia, Julia, Julia.* I wanna go, but I don't. I just don't. It's not that I want Papá to invite me, but…

Julia, come on, Papá calls me. And then I go. I fly. I get in bed with them. Mamá caresses my hair, Willy cuddles with Papá. Take us to have breakfast somewhere Papá, he tells him. Where can we go?

Los Tacos del Loco: closed.

La Mexicana: closed.

Gorditas La Feliz: closed.

Maybe La Nueva Central is open, I said.

Papá nodded, like he knew it was a good idea.

No, Mamá said, La Nueva Central is downtown, and there is no way we are going to downtown.

Everything, everything's been closing down in our city.

I can make French toast with Julia, Mamá says.

But I wanna eat out, we never do it anymore, Willy insists.

But Willy, our favorite places are now closed, don't you know?

But why? Why is everything closed down, Papá? Why is the whole city closing down little by little?

Well, because it is, I tell him.

But, but, I wanna eat out, I wanna be served a huge plate with food, and I want choco-milk, and I want juice and…

It is what it is, goddamn it! Papá stands up, gets dressed, and goes to the kitchen.

We hear him opening and closing cabinets, drawers, the fridge.

Let's go help Papá, Mamá says.

But I wanna eat OUUUUUT.

Willy, stop it.

We all get up, we help Mamá make her bed. When we get to the kitchen, breakfast is ready.

Are you making ham and eggs, Papá? I don't like ham and eggs, you know it.

Papá takes Willy's plate and throws his ham and eggs into the trash can. He says, Well, now you don't get to eat. Go to your room.

Mamá and I look at each other, and we start eating right away. It is really good, I tell Papá as I eat. He doesn't say a thing.

When I am done, I rinse my plate. I excuse myself and go to Willy's room. His door is closed, like everything else.

JUNE 11TH

I am so sad. Classes are over, and we all had to say goodbye to Tere. She is not coming back after summer is over.

We cried and cried and cried.

When Mamá picked me up, she said, What is wrong, Julia, why have you been crying?

I told her about Tere. She said she was sorry, she said that is what life is about.

Friends leaving? I asked.

No, she said, change.

I hate change.

Then I guess to cheer me up, Mamá told me that she had a surprise for us, that we had to guess.

But Willy could not guess. I could not guess. Tell us, we said.

The surprise is that for our first week of summer vacation, we are going to Tía's.

JUNE 15TH

Migra, Migra, **MIIIIIGRAAAAAA**, yells Jonás and we are all
running around trying to escape from him. Some of the kids
hide under cars, some hide behind trees, everyone tries to find
the best place to fool the Migra.

There are so many of us. The neighbors from the building
next to Tía's, three brothers and one sister that go from seven
years old up to fourteen. There's also the two girls that live
right across the street, they are twins, they are twelve and, as
Jonás says, together they make twenty-four. There's also the
kid whose mom runs the corner store, he is very quiet, but oh
boy does he run. There's also Willy, Jonás and me.

I am the Migra! yells Jonás as he pulls one of the twins out
from behind a gate. Show me your papers!

But the twin has no papers, so she is taken to detention.
She yells that she has papers, that her sister has them, but the
Migra is long gone. The rest of us try hard not to laugh so the
Migra does not get us.

Migra, Migra, Migra, Jonas yells and yells as he looks in all
the usual places. Ernie, the corner store boy, runs to detention.
He is trying to save one of the twins, but the Migra gets him.
Now the Migra needs to find the seven of us that are hiding
from him.

Jonás is a good Migra, he gets most of us, and puts us in
detention. Jonás is only missing one immigrant, my brother
Willy. We wonder where he is. We want him to save us.

Then, from the top of a tree, Willy jumps and runs, Migra,
Migra, I am here to get you, he says. Jonás misses Willy who
has arrived to free every single one of us from jail.

Good bye, Migra, good bye, we all tell Jonás who tries to get us with no luck. He gets mad. I don't wanna be the Border Police no more, he says. Plus, this is a kid's game, I am way too old for this.

We all boo him. I am serious, who wants to be next? No one wants to be the Border Police. But without Migra, there's no game.

Then, from inside Tía's house, Bis comes out and says, I can be the Border Police, and we continue playing.

I guess that it's not so bad that Bis is forgetting many things, because she is also forgetting how to be a great grandmother and she becomes one of us. See, I tell Jonás, if Bis can play with us even though she is almost a hundred years old, you can too.

Tía and Mamá are arguing about something. They mention Bis every other sentence. I don't understand if they are arguing about who wants her and who will not get her, or about who doesn't want her and will get her. Like she is a toy. I am sure Bis doesn't like to be passed around like a toy. I wonder if she really understands what is happening. I mean she is there, with them, but she doesn't say a thing. It's like she is not really there. She looks at them without looking at them. She does that all the time lately.

Out in Tía's backyard, I hear Willy and Jonás playing. I don't know exactly what they are doing. Jonás yells: Ready? Then he waits a few seconds before saying, Jump! and then I hear thump after thump. I hear Willy laughing. Oh, Willy, he can get so happy so easily.

Ready?...

JUMP!

Ready?...

JUMP!

After one or three jumps, I hear more thumps, but inside the house. The door opens and closes like in a second. It's our Bis. She left her chair and went out. I go after her and I see her all set, waiting for Jonás's instructions. She curls up and every time he yells **JUMP!**, she jumps, higher and higher. Come, come, she tells me, this is fun. We hold hands, we curl up, and then we jump.

We laugh and laugh and laugh. We laugh so hard all of

us, there we are all together curling up and then we all yell: Ready?… **JUMP!** again and again. We jump higher and higher. We laugh and laugh. We laugh and jump. Here we go again:

Ready?…

JUMP!

Ready?…

JUMP!

Repeat!

JUNE 16TH, THE AFTERNOON

What I like the most about El Paso is going shopping. And I don't even mean clothes and toys. I mean going grocery shopping. That I like, I like it so much. Everything is prettier, softer, yummier.

Mamá walks around with Tía, and us kids are in charge of pushing the cart. Willy sits inside, while Jonás and I take turns pushing or putting our feet on the cart and hanging off the front. We fly around the store, we yell, we laugh, we have fun. You two are too old for this, Tía tells us, but Jonás says Willy has a magic trick and makes us as young as he is. She smiles and says, If only.

We are kids, little kids, the three of us. The world disappears when we are together.

Sometimes I wish I could live here, no, not in El Paso, but in the supermarket with my brother and my cousin. We could live here for years eating all the food in every one of the aisles.

Kill me, kill me, **KILL MEEEEEEEEE**, I tell Jonás. **PUM, PUM, PUM**. Jonás kills me. I put my hands on my chest, I walk a few steps back, a few steps forward. How…how…how could you? I tell him gasping.

Slowly, so slowly, I let myself fall on the floor, I am losing it. I am breathless. I am the perfect actress.

Then, I die.

Tía would say we might be a little too old to play this, but, oh well.

Jonás comes close, his plastic gun in his hand. I don't know why you like being killed so much, Julia.

I don't know why I like it, but I do, I really like it. I like dying. I like staying still. My eyes open or my eyes closed, but still. I wait for Willy to make a siren sound, like an ambulance. I wait for Willy to be the paramedic who will try to bring me back to life.

~~I am sure that's how it will happen. I am sure that's how Pedro or Papá will die if they continue working with el Güero.~~

I should not have said that.

JUNE 20TH

Today Tía sent us to Sunday School with Jonás, Mamá tried to tell her we never go to church back home, but when Tía and Mamá argue, Tía always wins. So off we went. First we had to hear the whole service. I tried to count how many times people said the word God, but then I got tired.

When the service was over, while adults were talking to each other or eating some corn on the cob, us kids were sent to class. Our instructor was Miss Lee. She welcomed us to the house of God and then gave us a lecture about the beauty of paradise. Then she told us to draw paradise. She said we could draw it however we wanted. Everyone in class drew gardens, big trees, flowers, clouds, sun, butterflies, and birds all over.

I didn't.

My paradise was deep in the ocean. I drew a big fat golden fish swimming in the sea. My sea was humongous and blue blue blue. On one corner of the drawing, you can see a little sun. One of the girls in Sunday School told me that paradise is not like that. You are wrong, said another one. Miss Lee heard them and said, This can be paradise too because this is also a work of God our Lord.

I wanted to say that it was actually *my* work, but I didn't dare. Plus, Miss Lee was very nice to me and she said how much she liked *my* paradise.

I told Tía about it and she was very proud of me. She said, Miss Lee is right, everything is a work of God our Lord.

JUNE 21ST

So, today I saw IT—Jonás' peepee!

Truth is, I didn't wanna see it at first, but I was curious. Show you mine if you show me yours, he said. I had never seen a peepee, I mean I have seen my brother's, actually I see his all the time. But it's not the same to see your little brother's peepee than to see someone else's.

I first told him we shouldn't because we had just gone to Sunday School yesterday, but I was a bit curious. So we showed each other our private parts.

Do you wanna touch it? he asked me. I didn't.

He barely saw me, he didn't touch me either. It was like we both just wanted to get it over with in a second.

When we were done, I told him he could kiss me if he wanted to. I kissed you once, and you pushed me away, he said, then you didn't talk to me for days.

I won't push you this time.

Jonás kissed me and deep inside, I imagined it was Pedro, I imagined he held me with his big tattooed arms. I imagined he carried me in his arms.

Wouldn't you like to spend the summer here? asked Jonás, interrupting my daydream.

Summer here sounded great.

I think my mom would say, Yes, Julia. We only need to ask your mom.

Jonás told me that spending the summer together would be

great because we could go to the community center and swim everyday and bike and…

JULY 1ST

I hate Mamá. I really hate her.

I hate her so much even my nails hurt.

First, just when I was starting to have fun in El Paso, she dragged us back, only because Papá is coming back from his last trip. Even Willy got mad, and Willy never gets mad. Of, if he does, we don't know.

Why can't we stay in El Paso for the whole summer? I asked. You go and we stay. We promise to be good.

Willy said, Come on, Mamá, at least let us stay for the fireworks.

What fireworks? asked Mamá.

Fourth of July is around the corner, and Jonás told me there is a big celebration downtown and we want to go.

No, no, no, Mamá said, Papá won't like it.

But you promised. You promised we would have fun this summer, Willy insisted.

I told Willy to cut it out. There is no use, Willy, I said, she doesn't want us to ever have fun.

Mamá, why don't you do what you want? I do it all the time, it's fun, you will like it, Willy said.

Mamá only does what Papá wants, I said.

That is when it happened. She slapped me. It's been ages since she last did it, but it felt as if she had been practicing every single day.

Seriously, Julia, when did you become such a big mouth? she said.

I wanted to say that I was not a big mouth, I was just being honest, but I didn't. Also, I didn't cry, and believe me, I wanted to. I just stood there.

I hate her.

JULY 2ND

The fucking city is covered with these posters, Papá says. He is right, it's covered with these posters with photos of politicians who want you to vote for them. Fucking shitty candidates, Papá adds. None of them will be a good governor.

Do not say fucking, Mamá tells him.

Or shitty, I say.

Fucking women, they are all the same, aren't they, Willy?

My brother laughs, like he always does about any silly thing Papá says. Papá says silly things only when he's had a couple of beers.

And he has had more than a couple.

We are on our way to Papá's favorite restaurant, the only one that hasn't closed down. We are celebrating something about his job, I don't know what, I just know that we are supposed to be happy.

Mamá and Papá look like a boyfriend and girlfriend after school. They walk holding hands. They giggle. They kiss. Papá caresses her hair and calls her **MY BEAUTIFUL QUEEN**. I like seeing them like that.

Bis is with us. When we arrive at the restaurant, she says she wants a lime ice cream. Mamá tells her that they do not have lime ice cream here.

Only BBQ, Willy adds.

But I want, **I WANT**, I want lime ice cream, she says.

She is like a stubborn little girl who wants candies when you are not supposed to have candies. Mamá orders a limeade for Bis and that sorta calms her down. But then, like we are still talking about it, Bis says that Papá is right, the fucking city is covered with posters, with posters of girls, girls that are nowhere to be found, girls who have been taken away. Fucking shitty city we live in, she ends.

JULY 5TH

Today I got into yet another fight with Mamá. Details don't matter, what matters is how Willy is now getting into these things too. It went like this:

Mamá: I am really not enjoying your "I hate everything" phase. I mean, look at you, it seems that hate is your favorite word now.

Willy: What is an "I hate everything" phase?

Mamá: Willy, I am talking to your sister.

Willy: Ok, but first tell me what it means.

Mamá: What *what* means?

Willy: The "I hate everything" phase. Can I have one too?

Me: Wait a couple of years, I bet you will.

Mamá: Julia!

Willy: But I don't want to wait a few years.

Me: Well, I guess you can start now, do it with me, tell Mamá that you also hate being locked up at home.

Willy: I hate…

Mamá: …

JULY 7TH

I bet that if Bis reads my tarot now it will say, A long boring summer is ahead of you. And the card will be something like the card of the sun but with a very "I hate everything" face.

JULY 12TH

Mamá is taking me to the girl's doctor this week, all because I haven't gotten my period.

But you said everybody is different, I tell her.

Yes, but now it's taking too long and I am a bit worried, I just want to make sure that…you are fine.

That is her way of saying: I can't stand you, YOU argue about everything I say.

Yes, diary, I do that, in case you wonder.

I don't want to go to the girl's doctor, Mercedes once told that they see you naked down there. But who knows if it is true. I don't trust Mercedes all that much anymore.

Geez. I really don't wanna go to the doctor.

I don't wanna be naked down there. I don't wanna be a woman no more. I don't wanna have my period, it seems it is all way too hard.

JULY 17TH

Normally it is Mamá who freaks out with news like this, when she actually reads or watches the news, that is. But this time I am scared too. It seems that a car exploded in downtown yesterday.

A bomb.

A bomb in a car.

A bomb in a car downtown.

This city is shittier as time goes by.

Mamá panicked and called Papá, even though he tells her not to call him when he is away, just text. But she called, and Papá did not answer the first time.

Or the second.

Or the third.

Or the fourth.

Papá answered the fifth time Mamá called. He was pissed, this is my new favorite word, by the way. He was pissed, I could hear him yelling, and Mamá didn't have him on speaker or anything. This better be important, Celia, he said.

Mamá told him about the bomb and about how she is so scared all the time.

Get me Julia, Papá said.

I couldn't believe my ears. Papá never asks to talk to me when he is on the phone.

Julia, he said, are you scared?

Scared? I asked.

Yes, are you scared about the bomb in the car?

And even though I was scared to death, I said: Not really, no. I wanted to impress Papá. No, I am not scared at all, we are fine.

Well, tell your Mamá not to call me every time she is a chicken-shit.

Mamá
is
a
chicken
shit,
yes she is, yes she is.

JULY 18TH

Two things:

1. Papá
is
back.

AND

2. He looks like

SHIT

JULY 21ST

Mamá hates the telephone, she says that it only rings with bad news. I don't know what she means. We haven't had any bad news, have we?

Since Tere left and I stopped hanging with Mercedes, when the phone rings, it is never for me. It is either Tía, Papá, or Pedro on the other line. So imagine my surprise when it rang and Mamá said, Julia, it's for you.

It was Jonás. He said he called just to talk.

Me: Are you bored? Is that why you called me?

Jonás: No, I called you just because. But now that you ask, yes, I am a bit bored. Summer sucks. I never get to see my friends during the summer, Mamá is always working and Bis, well…what are you up to?

Me: Well, my summer is way worse than yours.

Jonás: How so?

Me: We are at home all-the-time.

Jonás: Really?

Me: Yes, and it sucks… I mean, at least you can go out and bike, we can't even set a foot outside our house.

Jonás: Well, that's the thing, I can't even bike. I got a flat and my mom's been way too busy to take me.

Me: Can't you fix it yourself?

Jonás: No, I can't.

Me: Why? Aren't boys and men supposed to be able to fix everything?

Jonás: Not everything.

Me: That sucks. You were my hope.

Jonás: Your hope?

Me: To fix *my* life.

Jonás: Julia, you are too crazy, I don't think anyone can fix you. You are like way too broken.

JULY 26TH

Well, elections happened a few weeks ago, but the city is a whole mess. No one is happy, there are protests everywhere. We can't leave the house, it's not safe, Mamá tells Tía on the phone.

I want to yell at Tía, we NEVER go out anyway. I am starting to believe...I am starting to think that this summer doesn't know it is summer.

I am starting to think that Califas does not know he is a cat.

I am starting to think that Mamá does not know how to be a mother.

I am starting to think that Papá does not know how to be a father.

I am starting to think that no one knows how to run this city.

This is my way of saying

everything

and everybody around me SUCKS.

AUGUST 1ST

Papá left again and this time Pedro had to go with him. Mamá will get all crazy and everything. She'll say:

DON'T answer the phone,
DON'T answer the door,
DON'T complain about my headaches.

Turn off the lights, Mamá says.
But it is only 8 pm, we tell her.
I don't care, turn it off, let's make them believe we are not here.

THEM WHO?

AUGUST 3RD

Dear Diary,

We've been watching a lot of TV. Mamá stays in her studio and doesn't even supervise us. It's like she doesn't even care what we do as long as we don't make a lot of noise. Or make her nervous. Or give her headaches.

Today we watched a movie about a girl who is just like me, minus the haircut and the clothes, and the attitude. I liked her name—Mathilda, like the one of that book, the one whose parents are so mean. I wonder if all the Mathildas in fiction suffer as much as these two.

But, back to the movie we watched.

Mathilda, just like the one in the book, has a family that sucks ass, they insult her, they hit her…but then they are killed, all of them, but she doesn't care about any of them except for her little brother. I have to admit that I did cry a little when he is shot. You wonder why she wasn't killed, right? Well, because she was out in the store, something I haven't done in ages because, you know, this city is not safe.

Anyway, her neighbor saves her, or sorta. His name is Leon and he is a professional killer—actually that is why the movie is called *The Professional*, so she begs him and begs him and begs him to teach her how to kill people, only you don't call it that, you call it cleaning.

The girl wants to avenge her family. She wants to clean for a living. It seems that shooting is not all that difficult, you just need to want it really bad.

Willy fell asleep as soon as the movie started, which was best because it was a bit creepy, like when she says to the hotel manager that Leon is her lover. Why would she say that?

Leon reminds me of Pedro. I know that Pedro would save me from anything and anyone.

Oh, and they are repeating this movie over the weekend, I am so gonna watch it again.

AUGUST 5TH

I hate everything, I hate my everything: Mamá, our house, the summer, my brother, Papá, Pedro… I hate everything and everyone.

Why? I don't know, I just do.

No, wait, I do know. I hate everything and everyone because we can't leave the house, because we can't go out, because we are stuck at home all day every day. What is the point of having money and a car if we can't do anything with either one of them?

I can't believe I'm going to say this, but I really want classes to start.

AUGUST 5TH, SAME BORING DAY

I watched *The Professional* again. Or tried to. Right after that
scene where the bad guys start shooting Mathilda's family,
Mamá said to turn it off. This is not for girls. It didn't matter
how many times I told her I had already watched it and it
wasn't all that scary, she still wanted me to turn it off.

At least this time, I had time to write down a dialogue
between Mathilda and Leon. The scene goes like this. He walks-
up the stairs and sees Mathilda who has a bloody nose because
her father hit her. Leon looks at her, I mean, he really looks at
her, then he gives her a tissue. She cleans her nose before she
says:

MATHILDA: Is it always like this or does it get easier when
you're older?
LEON: It is always like this. Just gotta deal with it.

No one in my family has ever hit me so hard that I end up
bleeding, but I know, I really know, how she feels. I wonder
if Leon was telling the truth: Life does **NOT** get easier as you
grow up.

AUGUST 7TH

Papá came back all messed up from his last trip. He looks skinnier, he's limping a bit, his face shows pain. He looks like a street dog that has just been hit by a car and pretends nothing happened.

He stays in his room all day long. Mamá takes him breakfast, lunch, dinner. Mamá takes him coffee, beer, coffee, beer.

We hear them talking, well, more like I hear them, Willy is always too busy shooting his toys with his new plastic gun.

Last night I heard them talking about the future.

Our future.

Papá told Mamá that maybe she is right. Maybe it's not a bad idea for us to move to El Paso.

Are you serious? she said. We will *all* go to El Paso?

No. Not all of us, he said.

Not all of us.

AUGUST 9TH

When we moved here, when Papá just got his job, he and Mamá would go to their room or send us to our rooms if they needed to talk adult stuff. Now, I don't think they even care if we are here or we are not, if we hear or if we don't.

Today, while we were eating lunch, Mamá said: Guillermo, I gotta tell you something. This morning when you left, I received a threatening call.

Papá just stood there. What do you mean?

They said...they said that they will get you.

Papá took a good look at Mamá. He took a good look at the three of us and I thought, Oh boy, here it comes.

And it sure did.

Papá pulled Mamá's chair close to him and said, Do you think, do you really think, *they* are gonna call to say *they* wanna get me?

Mamá shrugged.

Papá then pulled her face close—too close, so close to his—and said, LISTEN, if *they* wanna get ME, *they* would just do it, *they* would just FUCKING do it: without threats.

Mamá tried to pull away, but Papá pulled her back again and said, Don't YOU come and try to scare me with your stupid lies. I told you to leave! I told you to take the kids. I told you, didn't I? And did you? No, right, well, now just fucking grow a pair and cut the shit, you hear me?

I had a dream. I had a gun. A gun just like Papá's, only shinier. I had a gun in my hand and when *they* came, I was all ready for them. I was all set to shoot and kill them, one by one. There were so many of them, I couldn't see their faces, but I knew it was them. I knew it. One of them looked at me and said, She's just a girl.

But I wasn't just a girl in my dream, I was more than that, I was a girl with a shiny gun in her hand.

Some other guy asked me, Where is your father? And right when I was about to answer, Willy woke me up.

He was on top of me. I had a nightmare, he said, I had a nightmare, can I sleep with you?

And I said, Of course you can. Because Willy and I know that my parents' room is not a safe place any more.

AUGUST 10TH

I am not stupid. Not anymore.

I watched *The Professional* again, the whole movie.

It got me thinking about Papá.

He is involved in something fishy.

Who gets a car, money, a house, and papers to get a visa just like that?

Don't get me wrong. I like:

- the car
- the money
- the house
- everything he has gotten us

But. He wouldn't have gotten it just like that, just because, would he?

Plus he always comes back looking like shit. Today he looks like shit.

Papá is into something bad, something he is not supposed to be into.

I am not saying that I believe what Tere once said, that Papá is a narco. There is no way Papá is a narco, but yes, he must be into something fishy.

One of these days I will ask, I will simply go and ask. I mean, I deserve to know, right? He is my father after all and this is my family. I need to know. I must know.

I'm gonna go and tell him, Cut the shit, Papá, what are you up to?!

THREE

"Pienso en todo lo que voy perdiendo,
para quizá después recuperarlo."

Wendy Guerra, *Todos se van*

AUGUST 15TH

Much has happened in my life. I mean, it's been days of craziness! Here are some of the highlights:

1. I am not going back to school yet because of how things are.
2. When I say "how things are," I mean how things ARE in the city AND in my family.
3. A few here: the car bomb, the narcofosas, the protests about the elections, and the army scaring the shit out of everyone in Juárez.
4. Oh, yes, and what people are saying about Papá.
5. I asked Papá if it is true, if what people are saying about him and Pedro is true, and it only got me in trouble.
6. He said that things are not what they seem and that we are OK.
7. We are far from being OK.
8. Then, we had to move out from one day to the next. We left half our stuff behind.
9. We are living in a shitty house, the shittiest we've ever been in, the shittiest you can imagine. A place in which we are our own prisoners.
10. And then Papá left.
11. He's been gone more than usual.
12. Mamá keeps saying he will be back soon, but he hasn't even called, and he always calls.
13. Pedro hasn't called either.
14. So now Mamá keeps saying that maybe we should all go to El Paso and live with Tía until Papá and Pedro come back.
15. Yes, to El Paso.

AUGUST 17TH

Pedro is back, and he is our new babysitter now that Mamá spends day and night with Papá at the hospital. She comes, eats, takes a nap and then goes back, she doesn't say anything. She is like a ghost.

Yes, Papá is at the hospital. They haven't told us exactly what happened, but Pedro says he will be OK.

Tía will come this weekend. I wish she was here already. First, I didn't want to go to El Paso, but now I can't wait to get out of here. I don't wanna be in this old ugly house, and I don't wanna be in this stupid city that has done nothing but take things from me. Like my parents.

AUGUST 18TH

We were watching TV with Pedro, Willy was changing the channels, one after the other. He stopped and yelled when he saw a picture of our father on the screen. **LOOK**, look, he said, it's Papá, it's Papá, look, look! In less than a second, Pedro took the remote out of Willy's hand and changed the channel.

But it is Papá, Willy said.

Why was he on TV? I asked.

And because Pedro thinks I am an idiot, a stupid little girl who knows nothing, he said: Oh, he is there because everyone in the city is worried about him.

Yeah, right.

AUGUST 19TH

Because I can't take care of you two and take care of Papá at the same time.

Because Tía and Bis and Jonás will make sure you are all right.

Because things over here are way too hard now for you to handle.

What do you mean too hard now? Mamá, they have always been hard.

Oh, Julia. It just needs to be like this.

Because everything is dangerous here.

Because staying at home is dangerous.

Because going out is dangerous.

Because walking on the sidewalk is dangerous.

Because staying home alone is dangerous.

Because one day even breathing is gonna be dangerous.

But what do you mean by dangerous, Mamá? Willy asks.

Oh, Willy. It just is.

It simply is.

I can't take care of you two.

Papá's health comes first.

So you two go because I say so.

Because you say so?

Yes. So, pack everything.

What do you mean by everything?

Everything.

But we have nothing, you made us leave everything back home.

Well, pack whatever you have.

Pack, just pack.

Pack whatever.

Whatever.

AUGUST 20TH

One diary.

One whole diary lost.

One too many weeks lost.

All gone.

Why? Because while we were packing, Mamá saw my diary and read everything I wrote about Papá and thought it might be dangerous. Evidence, she called it. I don't understand, I don't think I wrote anything, you know, dangerous.

She let me have my old diaries, the ones I wrote when I was twelve and a couple of those I wrote when I was thirteen, the ones I don't like to read all that much. They are so stupid. I was so stupid.

Stupid.

Maybe she is right, writing a diary is stupid.

But I can't help it. I need to write, there is nothing else to do.

First Mamá said, No more diaries for you, you are too old for them and you are so careless about what you say. Then she changed her mind, she thought keeping a diary would keep me busy. Later she was all over me asking and asking and asking what I was writing. Finally she said it, Why do you need to write? Writing is stupid.

Like painting? I said, and she slapped me.

Whatever.

What is the point anyway? No matter how much I write, it won't change the fact that Papá is now in the hospital, and our whole lives are a mess.

I have not lost a diary, I have lost my life, I have lost everything and no one seems to care, so no more writing for me, no more diary for me.

AUGUST 20TH, AFTERNOON

OK, I know I said I would not write anymore, but Tía, as soon as we got in the car, gave me this new diary, no matter how many times I told her Mamá didn't want me to write. She said, Keep it, write. You can write while you're in the car on the bridge. Besides, she said, a diary is a good place to say what you feel.

I guess Tía is right, my diary is the only place where I get to say what I feel. So, that is it, I will write. I will write everything I feel.

Once I figure out what I feel, of course.

AUGUST 20TH, NIGHT

When Tía sets us up, she puts Willy and me in the same room even though I told her I couldn't share a room with Willy...Tía tells me to cut it out. She reminds me to thank God we are all together now and that we all have a roof over our heads.

I can sleep with Mamá, I say.

Tía does not reply. Then she says, We'll see about that when she comes.

And when is **THAT** going to happen? I ask.

Tía clams up. Just like Mamá.

They say teenagers stop talking to their families. They say teenagers keep secrets, hide things. I guess Mamá and Tía are the teenagers in this family.

At night, while we are all having dinner, I ask, How long will we be staying here anyway?

Tía stares at her soup.

Answer me, I say.

Don't talk to me like that, Julia.

Well, then tell me when Mamá is coming.

Don't raise your voice, Tía says.

Then talk to me.

Tía clears her throat and says, A while, at least, at least until your father gets better.

I wanna tell her, But he is never gonna get better, never, he is a dead man who just happens to have a beating heart. But I don't, I don't say anything because Willy doesn't need to know that. Not just yet.

AUGUST 21ST

So, here I am with a brand new diary for a brand new life.

First I thought, I will write it all again, all over again. I will write everything that happened to us. What happened in our neighborhood, what happened after the elections. What happened to Papá. Of course, I wanted to write about what happened to Papá.

But, I don't wanna live it all again. Because writing is living things all over again, at least that's what my composition teacher used to say in school.

Back when I was in school.

I didn't even get to say goodbye to Mercedes or Pepe or René. Or Tony.

Tony. I think that I will never see Tony again.

You probably wonder who Tony is.

You wouldn't be asking who Tony is if Mamá hadn't gotten rid of my other diary. Tony was a main character there and now Mamá knows about him, she knows it all. Not that she cares.

She cares about nothing but Papá.

Papá, nothing but Papá.

I also care about Papá, but he is not the only person in my mind, like he is for Mamá. It's like she has forgotten that she has two kids. No, it's me who has a kid. My brother is now my kid. Or something like that. I mean Tía takes care of both of us, but Tía also takes care of many other things.

So, Willy is my business now.

Willy often looks at me and asks, When is Mamá coming? When is Papá going to be OK?

I tell him, Soon, very soon, Willy.

But I am lying to him the same way Mamá is lying to us when she calls and says she will be back soon, very soon.

AUGUST 24TH

My birthday's around the corner and obviously a party is out of the question.

Whatever, birthdays are stupid. Tía says that we can have dinner at the buffet Bis likes.

A party in a buffet, how about that?

You can invite whoever you want, she says.

Who am I going to invite? I don't know anybody but her and Jonás and Bis in this city. I tell her so.

Well, that is because school hasn't started, but once it does, you will make friends. You are good at making friends.

Yeah, I am, but I am good at making friends in Spanish, not in English. Besides, who will want to go to celebrate in a buffet? Not me, that's for sure.

AUGUST 25TH

Because Willy has been all quiet and sad, Tía gives him a five-dollar bill. What am I gonna do with it? he asks. Tía then tells Jonás to take him to the store to buy anythinghewants. I tag along.

I guess we have to make sure that anythinghewants is worth exactly five dollars, right?

Tía gives me a look and then hands me an extra five-dollar bill. You buy yourself something too.

We walk down the street. Willy walks fast, ahead of us, he is singing and jumping, and fooling around already happy for the candies he hasn't even seen.

Jonás: So, how did you sleep last night?

Me: Fine, I guess.

Jonás: Do you like your new room?

Me: I don't care.

Jonás: It used to be our TV room, that is why now the TV is in the dining area. I like it better there, we can eat and watch TV.

Me: Whatever.

Jonás: Whatever, that is all you say lately.

Me: Whatever.

Jonás: Are you OK? I mean, after everything that happened? Were you scared? What exactly happened?

Me: You are asking too many questions.

Jonás: What does he look like, your dad? You know, in the hospital.

Me: I dunno.

Jonás: How come?

Me: Well, they don't let me—they don't let *us*—see him, they say we are too young.

Jonás: Damn, he's the first one in our family to get killed.

Me: He's still alive, asshole!

Jonás: Oh, yes, of course, I meant, because, it is just that…

Me: He's not dead, he is not dead, he is not dead. Papá's alive, he's just—he just doesn't look alive. But he'll get better and everything will go back to normal and we'll go back home and…

Even I can't believe my own lies. Even me.

AUGUST 26TH

I thought that the one good thing about living with Tía would be being around Bis. But she is at her worst.

- She seasoned our scrambled eggs with sugar, instead of salt.
- She dropped two glasses of chocolate milk.
- She called me Lilia instead of Julia.
- She asked Willy more than two times if he wanted breakfast, even though we had already eaten breakfast.
- Oh, and she still refuses to take a shower.

Tía tries to pretend this is Normal-Bis, to forget stuff, to get mixed up, but I am sure that deep down she knows Bis is not herself. Why else would she pray more and more every night? I hear her, Holy Father this, Holy Father that.

AUGUST 26TH, NIGHTTIME

Poor Tía, she has to take care of all of us, and by all of us I mean Bis, Mamá, Jonás, Willy, me, and all of her patients in the hospital. I heard her talking to one of our neighbors, who said to Tía, I don't know how you do it.

I don't either. Poor Tía.

She is like everybody's mother. I remember how many times Mamá would call her because Papá and her had argued and stuff. Hours and hours of them on the phone. Tía is so loud that even though she wasn't talking to me, I could hear her telling Mamá to calm down, to take it easy.

Bis once told me that since they were both little and their mother left, Tía was always taking care of Mamá. I have often wondered how it feels to have an older sister. One who takes care of you when everyone else has left you.

AUGUST 27TH

Tía is taking me to El Paso High School to register today. She says school starts late this year.

Whatever.

But I'm not in high school, I tell her, I am in middle school. She tells me that here in the U.S., ninth grade is high school, not middle school. I guess she sees my face all scared because she tells me that I should be super-excited because now I will be in the big kids' school. So cool, she says.

But it is not cool. It is fucking scary, only I don't tell her.

You will like it, she says, you will have classes in English and classes in Spanish. You will also get a locker and new friends and music lessons, and you can join the soccer team or the basketball team or...

I don't care what Tía says,

I don't want to be here.

AUGUST 27TH, NIGHTTIME

Mamá called tonight asking if we were OK and if I was ready for my new school. I told her, Of course we are OK, but not thanks to you. She pretended not to hear me, and then she asked again about school.

I said, Do you even care about us? We haven't seen you in ages.

Mamá told me she understood that I was upset, but I had to realize what the situation was. I told her I had realized it long ago and way better than she did.

Julia, she said, why do you have to be so difficult?

Because you left us, Mamá.

Mamá did not say anything, I could hear her breathing, I could even hear her heart beating, pum, pum, pum. I could hear words trying to come out of her lips and how her lips closed up again, like a clam.

How is Willy? she asked.

He is OK, he misses you, wanna talk to him?

AUGST 27TH, SO LATE EVEN THE CRICKETS ARE SLEEPING

Willy says that the only thing he doesn't like about El Paso is that Mamá and Papá are not here. But everything else is great. How come? I asked. He looked at me as if I was from another planet. Julia, EVERYTHING, look:

- The parks are clean.
- People walk their dogs.
- I even saw a lady walking her cat!
- The stores have Mexican candies and American candies.
- There is a firemen station in every corner.

No, there isn't, I said. He looked at me and gave me a look as if he was saying, Fine, you are right. But then he added, but I have never seen firemen back home and here you even see them buying Coca-Colas.

And my school, have you seen my school?

Willy likes that his school looks like a house, he likes that it is all covered and that it has halls and that he will get a chair and a desk just for himself. Willy likes how all the teachers decorate their classrooms with many more things than back home.

Aren't you nervous that everyone will speak English except you? I ask, and the minute I say it I regret it. Me and my big mouth.

No, I am not. I will learn. Tía says that us kids learn everything faster.

I guess Willy is right. When did he become the smart one in the family?

What I miss the most about home is Tere. I know she left almost a year before we did. I know I was hanging out with Mercedes more in those last months. But then Mercedes and I got into a fight. Also, Mercedes wasn't as cool as Tere after all.

I miss Tere, I do. I miss her a lot.

I am sure she will understand what I am going through. And I am sure I will never get a friend like her.

If I knew where she was, if I had her phone number, I would call her and tell her that I am about to start high school even though back home I am still in middle school. I would tell her I am shitting my pants just by thinking about it. I would tell her that what makes me even more nervous than speaking English in all of my classes is the clothes, yes, the clothes.

What about the clothes, Tere would ask?

And I would tell her what I have heard, that clothes in high school matter, clothes help you fit in or become the reason no one ever talks to you.

And Tere, Tere would tell me not to worry, Tere would remind me that as always, I am overreacting.

I will never find another Tere like Tere.

AUGUST 29TH

I've been thinking a lot. At first, I thought that by taking us out of our house and our family and our country, our mother had kicked us out of her life.

But really, she kicked us out of ourselves. She kicked us out of childhood, the little childhood I still had left.

Now we are like dogs without owners who are trying hard to be cute and funny so someone can love them. Nevertheless, instead of being like stupid dogs without owners, we—Willy and me—we should be more like stray cats who don't give a fuck about owners and petting and just live to survive.

Mamá says she is coming this weekend, but I don't believe her. Even if she comes, she will just pet us for a second and then she will be gone again.

SEPTEMBER 1ST

It is still the same with Mamá, exactly the same. Why am I even surprised or even mad? It is just plain and simple, us kids, *her* kids, are not as important to her as Papá.

SEPTEMBER 2ND

Tía took Bis to the doctor, so Jonás and I are in charge of Willy who is bored to death.

Jonás says that we should all tell horror stories since Tía is not here. Come on, like we used to do when we were little.

We are still little, Willy says.

Oh, come on, let's do it, let's. I am just gonna start. Once upon a time.

We have always done this, you know? Telling horror stories. We used to do it with Pedro in the car or at home. I don't like telling horror stories with Jonás though. In his stories there are no ghosts, vampires or zombies. In his stories there are only bad, very bad men, just men with no powers but still they do horrible things like cut people's throats, heads, bury them while still alive or light them on fire right in front of their family.

It's like as soon as he starts telling a story, Willy runs away. They're that bad.

I wanna go too, I wanna go run away too, but if I do he will say I am just a baby, and he will be calling me baby and some other names all weekend. So I stay.

He tells the story of Viri, a girl who was from whoknowswhere and who used to work at this factory where she was more like a slave, but one day just because she said NO to her boss who wanted to take her out, she was raped and killed.

It's true, I am not inventing this, Jonás says.

It's my turn now. I breathe in, breathe out while trying to come up with a story that sounds as scary as his, I want to come up with a story that freaks him out SO much that he never wants us to tell horror stories ever again.

Once upon a time, there was this little boy who would touch his peepee all the time, so much that one day…

No, that's not a horror story, Julia, come on.

Once upon a time, there was this old abandoned house. No one would dare even look at it because…

Oh, come on, we all know stories about abandoned houses. Why don't you…why don't you tell me the story of how your Dad was killed?

Stupid, Papá wasn't killed, I've told you so.

But someone tried to. I am sure someone is still trying to kill him.

I don't wanna play this game anymore. I am going with Willy.

I sit down in front of the TV next to my brother. Why are you crying? he asks me. Jonás scared you with his stories too?

Yes.

Willy hugs me and then puts my head in his lap, like Mamá used to do with Papá when he came home tired and messy from work.

If Mamá has Papá, I have Willy.

SEPTEMBER 3RD

Tía took us to buy stuff for school. I asked her if she could get me a new diary and she said, But I just gave you one, are you done with it? I told her yes, even though I haven't. But I want a diary that is less childish.

Ok, we'll get you one, but be careful.

Careful how?

Just careful, she said, with what you write.

I was about to say something when she added, You know how your mother gets, so either be careful with what you say or be careful where you place it.

I like Tía.

So here I am writing in a diary that is not pink and doesn't have little stars all over it. Here I am writing in my new diary, but being careful about it, so careful that I will not write that sometimes I wish Papá was dead so that Mamá finally would come back for us, or that sometimes I wish Papá **AND** Mamá died so we could be free of them and their bullshit. I am so careful that I am not gonna write that sometimes I wish that I was the one connected to all those tubes half alive and half dead so that my parents were the ones feeling like shit.

Yes, I am careful with my diary, I am not writing anything that could hurt anyone except me.

SEPTEMBER 3RD, VERY LATE, BUT CRICKETS ARE STILL AWAKE

Sometimes I just want the nights to go by quick, I want them to last like a second. But they don't, they last many, too many, hours.

No.

More like centuries. Nights last centuries since we moved, and I spend every one of them with my eyes wide open and everything, everything runs around in my mind.

Everything that we don't have anymore. Everything we are not anymore.

But tonight, tonight I am not thinking about *that* everything. Tonight I am thinking that in a couple of days, school starts. My very first day in high school and I am so scared.

What if I fail at being in high school? What if everybody hates me? What if, what if, what if?

I wish I could wake up Bis, so she can read me her tarot and tell me my future.

SEPTEMBER 4TH

I took one of Tía's lipsticks and painted my lips.

I stood there, in front of the mirror. I stared at me, I stared at my lips. I stood there until I got used to the new me.

I am a new me.

I have spent the whole weekend getting ready for my first day of high school. I've been putting all the clothes Tía bought me on the bed to mix and match this and that. Capris or jeans? Flowery blouse or funky t-shirt? Tennis shoes or sandals?

One thing is sure, figuring out what to wear and what my hair should look like is not easy. I want to look great, but I don't want people to think that it took me hours to get there.

Geez, I get more and more scared as the hours pass by.

Monday is almost here and I am so not ready for it.

SEPTEMBER 5TH

OK, it is 6 pm. In fourteen hours or so this whole thing starts.

I have emptied my red backpack three times already. First, I filled it with all my notebooks and binders, but then I thought, I don't need everything all at once, do I? So, I took all of them out and just kept one notebook, one pen and one pencil. But then my backpack felt way too light.

Should I take you with me, dear diary?

SEPTEMBER 5TH

It is 9 pm. I am in bed, but I obviously can't sleep. Tía just came with a few reminders:

- Bring your ID
- Have your schedule in hand
- Be nice to everyone, but not too nice
- Don't forget to pick up your books
- Don't forget the lock for your locker

My locker! I don't remember where it is or what the number is. Oh my god, what am I gonna do?

Jonás must have heard me because he yelled from his room, The locker number is on your schedule and the lockers for all freshmen are on the first floor.

Are all my classes also in the first floor? I yelled back at him.

Check your goddamn schedule, he yelled back.

Don't say goddamn, Tía says. And stop yelling!

SEPTEMBER 5TH

It is midnight and I can't sleep. I can feel my anxiety growing inside of me. Will my nerves ever calm down?

I just wish that the first day of school would hurry up and come so that I can get it over with.

SEPTEMBER 6TH

It is over, the first day is finally over, thank god. When we were walking to school, I thought my insides would fall out of my butt, seriously.

Jonás started getting mad because I was asking so many questions. Just act as if you've been doing this your whole life, don't look surprised, play cool.

Is that what you did on your first day? I asked.

Actually, he said, on my first day, I tripped while going from one class to another, right there in front of everyone. I was a joke for weeks.

He made his best friend meet us by the door, so we could walk in all together. Her name is Patty, she is very nice. It is hard to believe that my Jonás' best friend is a girl. I wonder if deep down he likes her-likes her. She had on a cute skirt with a funny t-shirt, and I felt really underdressed. We walked through the doors, and I felt like all the other kids were looking at me because I was the new girl.

But then I sat down in my first class and the teacher made us play this game to introduce ourselves to each other. I could finally relax because I found out everyone else was just as new as I was.

Now looking back, I feel dumb for being that scared for the first day. Well, we'll see how it goes tomorrow.

SEPTEMBER 7TH

Mamá called to ask about our first week of classes. Willy got on the phone first. He told her that at school, kids get breakfast and lunch and books for free. He told her that some kids ride the bus, but not us because we live so close. He told her about music class and P.E. and how he is not the only one who speaks Spanish, he told her that almost everybody else speaks both English and Spanish. That is when I yelled to add in that not almost EVERYONE else speaks English and Spanish, but Willy ignored me, and he went on about his new teacher and his new friends and how much he loved his new school.

Willy is way too easy to please.

When it was my turn, I just said fine to everything she asked me.

How do you feel?

Fine.

How was your week?

Fine.

How do you like your new school?

Fine.

Have you been eating well?

Fine.

Did Tía tell you we are meeting soon?

Fine.

Why are you like this?

Fine.

Fine.

SEPTEMBER 8TH

Tía is pretty cool, even though she makes us pray before every dinner. Jonás is funny. Bis is always Bis.

So we are OK living here. But there are things I don't like. Things I almost hate:

- I don't like that I have to ask permission and say please and thanks all the time.
- I don't like, I almost hate, that I don't have a room of my own, I can't talk on the phone for hours with my friends because, well, I still don't have friends here.
- I don't like, almost hate, that we have to go to church every Sunday so early in the morning.
- I don't like, I almost hate, that we have to say things like: God willing, God bless you, God-given right, God forbid, God rest your soul and many others to every little thing we say.
- I don't like, really hate, that Mamá doesn't call doesn't come isn't here. Not that I want her to, I just hate that she doesn't.

SEPTEMBER 9TH

I got lost.

Just like that.

You see, Jonás stayed at home because he was sick. So, after class, I had to walk by myself to Tía's. I was pretty sure I knew my way back, I mean I had been walking to and from school for almost two days. But I guess I didn't know my way back. I walked out of school, I crossed the street and began to walk straight home like always. Then I turned right or turned left or maybe I went all the way around, I don't know.

I just got lost.

I was distracted maybe. I remember I was thinking of how much I like Mily's Vans, I was thinking that high school is pretty cool after all. I was thinking that I had fun at P.E. and that next year I wanna be part of the band and play the biggest instrument.

I was thinking about Papá.

I was thinking about Mamá.

I was thinking about my school back home.

I was thinking about my old house, my old city, that you can still see if you stand on tip toes on the balcony of Tía's house.

And I got lost.

I walked back and forth on the same street like three times. I sat down on a bench in the park. A guy was there, an old guy. A homeless guy. He asked me, Are you lost, girl?

And I wanted to say yes, but if I said yes, he could've done something to me. I said, No, I am not lost. I am just hanging out.

The homeless guy simply said, Do you have a dollar to spare? I am hungry.

I was hungry too. I gave him a dollar.

He said, Thank you, and I hope you find whatever you are looking for.

How did he know I had lost my way back, myself, and everything in my life?

I stayed on that bench for a while, it was a nice park after all, a silent park, but silent as any park can be right before the storm comes, and when I say the storm I mean the time all the kids that come and play and yell and…anyway, I left before the storm came and tried to find my way back until I did, I don't know how I did, but I did.

It was almost 6 pm.

As soon as I touched the doorknob, my Tía opened the door and slapped me hard across my face.

Where were you? I was worried sick, what's wrong with you? What took you so long?

I got lost. I got lost.

You said you could walk back home on your own.

Yes, but…

What if something had happened to you?

But nothing happened.

What the hell would I tell your mother if something had happened?

Bis was sitting on the couch. Leave her the fuck alone, she said.

I am sorry, I am sorry, please don't be mad, Tía.

You are just a girl, you know what happens to little girls these days?

That's in Juárez, I said.

No, that is everywhere.

Here too?

Yes, here too, everywhere, girls are never safe.

I am sorry. I said I am sorry, I just got lost, I got lost lost lost lost. Lost.

Bis, who is lately just quiet, stood up and held me in her arms and told Tía to cut it out. She just got lost, it can happen to anyone. You never got lost before?

SEPTEMBER 9TH

I just realized that there is one big difference between Juárez and El Paso. Over there, houses are stuck together, all the houses share walls with other houses. It doesn't matter how big or how small your house is, they are glued together. It's like they lean on each other or else they can't stand on their own.

Houses here don't need each other. Just like people here, it seems no one needs anyone else. There is so much space between houses, like they don't even wanna touch each other. It's like they all got in some fight, and now they ignore each other. Mind your own business, they say.

Well, I have seen houses leaning on each other like back at home, but those houses are in neighborhoods that are not pretty, neighborhoods that even God doesn't visit. I guess that it is exactly because God doesn't visit them, that they need to be so close to each other. Houses are like people, they need to lend each other a hand from time to time.

SEPTEMBER 10TH

So, tomorrow is my birthday. How are we celebrating? Well, we are going to a buffet just like Tía promised.

Tía and Bis and Willy are excited. Jonás and I suggested we at least go to Peter Piper Pizza, to play games and stuff. Tía said she would think about it.

SEPTEMBER 11TH

We did go to the buffet. BUT Tía also took us to this place with games, go-carts, mini-golf…and I must admit it was great after all. Happy birthday to me.

SEPTEMBER 12TH

I was curious and went to get my old diaries. The ones Mamá let me keep, of course.

I read them one by one. I was such a dumbass. I have all these stupid things about fighting with Mamá, about lipsticks and movies and vacation. Oh, and I made entries about school and friends and, I don't know…stupid shit.

The most stupid shit.

I need to start writing as a girl who has grown up.

Because I HAVE GROWN UP!

Damn it.

SEPTEMBER 18TH

So news is that we are changing religions or something. Tía met some ladies a few weeks ago, and they all became friends, and they asked her to come visit their church. She said yes. Like it isn't bad enough that we have to go to church all the time. Now we have two churches to go to.

Bis is angry. She is not as religious as Tía, but she does say that God is God, and he only invented one church. Tía says she agrees, but in these times you need all the help you can get from God, you need to find more places where God actually talks to you.

I wonder what Tía wants God to tell her.

This other church does not look like a church. It looks like a garage. It is full of plastic chairs, those chairs that you only take to picnics or kid's parties. There is nothing on the walls, there are no windows telling stories of the Saints, there are no sculptures with saints and women looking at God. No, there is no decoration at all. The priest is not called Priest, he is called Shepherd and he wears regular clothes, he has a microphone in his hands and says that in this place, we will only discuss God's Best-Seller. Everyone laughs except me and Willy. Tía looks at me and whispers: God's Best-Seller is the Holy Bible.

I still don't understand the joke.

I don't like going to church, but I prefer our old church over this place. I liked looking at the paintings, the sculptures of saints and virgins. I liked it because the priest looks like a priest and even though he says we are all living in constant sin, he also says that God takes care of us. He invites us to pray. He says every time we pray we make miracles. He asks us to pray for our brothers and sisters that live in this city. He asks us to pray for the ones who live beyond the border. He asks us to pray for people on both sides of the border. He also asks us to pray for our brothers and sisters who get lost when looking for the American Dream. He asks us to pray for everyone around us.

My favorite part in our regular church is when we shake hands with everyone. We shake hands with the people in our family. We shake hands with the people standing behind us. We shake hands with the people in front of us. Shake. Shake. Shake.

Maybe if we all shook hands, everything will be better.

SEPTEMBER 21ST

Tía says she wants to make a **Lady** out of me. She says it like that with a capital L. She says it in bold: A **Lady.**

But I don't want to be a lady. What for?

SEPTEMBER 23RD

I hate it when Mamá says soonverysoon.

    I will come and see you both soonverysoon.

    Everything will be back to normal soonverysoon.

    Papá will be OK soonverysoon.

    We will all be together soonverysoon.

    You will both come back home soonverysoon.

    You will both go back to your old schools soonverysoon.

    Soon.

    Very.

    Soon.

    Soonverysoon.

    I hate it, I hate it when she says that, especially because those soonverysoons never ever happen. Those soonverysoons are so slow, like they are inching across a huge, never-ending desert.

SEPTEMBER 25TH, WAY TOO EARLY

I heard Tía talking on the phone. I heard only her side of the conversation, but it went something like this:

- He is just there, yes, he is in a vegetative state.
- No, she doesn't know.
- She *is* hopeful.
- Yes, she is there all the time.
- Right, can you imagine?
- Oh, those journalists don't even know what they are talking about, all they want is to sell papers.
- They are clueless, completely clueless. Well, Willy is.
- Oh, he is such a sweet little boy.
- Julia is different. But she is adapting.
- Her? Well, it's hard to tell. She can be quite a piece of work. She's just like her mother.
- How is she? I wouldn't even know where to start.
- She's lost it.

Yeah, she was talking about us. She called Willy sweet. I guess she is right about Willy too, he is sweet. But I don't believe I am *quite a piece of work*. She said I was just like Mamá. Of course I am just like Mamá, she is my mamá after all.

What I didn't understand is what she meant when she said *She's lost it*. Who was she talking about? Mamá? If she was talking about Mamá, what has Mamá lost?

How do you lose yourself? I dunno. I stopped understanding

the rest of Tía's conversation until she said: They are my sister's children and they are staying with me.

She said it as if she really really loved us a lot, as if she would never dare to leave us all alone like Mamá did when this whole thing with Papá happened.

SEPTEMBER 25TH, STILL TOO EARLY

Sometimes I imagine I am all alone in the world. I imagine I have no one no one no one. I imagine that all there is left for me is to write and write and write in my diary until my fingers hurt, until my eyes close. Write and write and write until everything melts out there. I am going to write and write and write until I forget how to write.

Just like Bis.

SEPTEMBER 25TH

We are still going back and forth from one church to another and I still can't tell the actual difference.

OCTOBER 2ND

I am shaking, my mind is all over the place, my heart…

See, earlier today Jonás and me were at the corner store, buying snacks to watch a movie, then Jonás saw the newspaper, it read: *La Comadreja's Hit Man: Between Life and Death.*

That's Tío, said Jonás.

Who?

But then I saw the photo, and I saw Papá. Papá on a hospital bed with a bunch of things above his face. I took the newspaper, and we both read the whole thing, until we were told that we had to pay to read the paper. But Jonás said, Let's go, come on.

We didn't talk about it on our way home. We didn't talk about it at home. We didn't say anything about it to Tía or Bis.

Later that day I looked for my dictionary. I wanted to know what it said about the word hit man.

hit·man.
- n. a person who is paid to kill someone, especially for a criminal or political organization.
- synonyms: assassin, killer, murderer, gunman, hired gun, "he was paid to be a hit man for the Mafia."

Papá was a hit man just like Leon in that movie I watched so many times back when we were home. A hit man. Papá, a hit man.

Now it all makes sense. The gun. His travels. The police coming to look for him at home. The police taking our home apart. Mamá telling them she had no husband, telling them her husband was long gone. Mamá telling them he had abandoned her and her kids. The police taking Mamá with them.

Then Papá being at the hospital and no one explaining what had exactly happened to him.

I went to Jonás, Did you know about it? Did you already know about it?

About what, Julia?

Did you know Papá was a hit man?

No, he said, not really, kinda.

But who is this Comadreja, I asked. Papá doesn't work for him, he works for el Gringo. El Gringo, I said. Jonás looked at me and said, I don't know, maybe el Gringo works for La Comadreja, or maybe el Gringo is La Comadreja or something. I don't know.

You do know, I said, and I forced him to tell me everything. He didn't say much, he really didn't know much. He said he heard Tía talking on the phone. I told him I hear Tía talking about us all the time, but never about Papá.

Well, I heard her only once, she said that Tío was not that honest, she said…Julia, are you listening to me? Julia, don't cry. It's OK, you are OK, you will be with us from now on, we will take care of you. I will take care of you, you are my favorite girl-cousin after all.

Stupid Jonás, I am his only girl-cousin.

Hearing Jonás saying that he will take care of me made me think of Pedro. Pedro used to say he would always take care of me.

OCTOBER 3RD, LATE AT NIGHT

Pedro.

Is Pedro a hit man too?

OCTOBER 6TH

I've had this headache since yesterday that does not let me think or that is making me think more than usual. I've been feeling like shit. I wish I could just stay in bed forever, cover myself from toes to head and sink in.

Tía comes in and asks me what's wrong? I say nothing, but she knows everything. She gets in bed with me, she says nothing, but she says everything. Tía holds me, she holds me tight.

Finally, after I don't know how many minutes that feel like days, she says, You can stay home today if you want. You can stay in bed today if you want. But don't stay here to cry and pine away, stay here and gather strength because life goes on.

Life goes on, she says.

OCTOBER 8TH

Can you write a letter for me? Willy asked me today.

A letter? Who's it to?

Papá.

And so I did.

Dear Papá,

Get better already. Please come back. Just do it. I want you to walk out of that hospital and take us all back to our old house. You can always just tell Pedro or Mamá to take us back so we can all wait at home til you are back with us.

Come on, Papá, just get better. I promise to be good.

Your son,

Willy

[I wanted, I wanted SO BAD, to add a footnote, a long very long, oh, so long footnote telling Papá so many things, asking him so many other things, making sure he understood exactly how I am feeling after all that has happened over the last months, but I didn't. I did not dare to write a footnote on the letter that no one will ever read].

OCTOBER 11TH

Tía says Pedro called today. He wanted to say hi to us. He will call again later today, she said. We'll see. Willy says *whatever*, but I am really excited. After we are done with homework and chores, I sit down next to the telephone and wait for his call.

I will ask him what he has been doing now that we are not around. Then…then I will go straight to business. I will ask him about Papá. I will ask him if it is true what they say about Papá in the newspaper. I will ask him if it is true Papá killed all those people. I will ask him if it is true that Papá kidnapped all those people. I will ask him if he is a hit man too. But I know, I know he will say no. Pedro will say everything is a lie, and I will be very happy.

OCTOBER 16TH

There were a lot of people walking away from the bridge at the
border. All of them were carrying a lot of things, some of them
had happy faces, some of them looked worried. None of them
looked like Mamá. But then Willy said, *There she is, there she is!*
He ran to her. Mamá, Mamá, Mamá. He hugged her. Mamá was
carrying a little suitcase.

Tía asked me, Aren't you going to hug her too?

Later, I said.

I am sorry I missed your birthday, Mamá said.

You did miss it, I told her.

Mamá and Willy looked like one of those sculptures in
church, the Virgin Mary carrying baby Jesus close so close that
they almost become one. Mamá kissing him everywhere. My
boy, my Willy boy.

They walked toward us. I saw her and I knew I was
supposed to welcome her, but I didn't feel like it. I knew she
was going to say something like, I missed you so much, but still
I wasn't going to hug her.

Come on, go say hi to your mother.

I could see Mamá's tears on her face. Maybe she did miss us.

When she was right in front of me, she said, My God, you
have grown so much! You are not a little girl anymore.

That was it. That was all I needed. I felt something huge
coming out of my throat. I felt fire on my skin. She came close
to me, to kiss me. I guess that's when I did it. I slapped her. I
slapped Mamá.

Tía shouted, Julia! What are you doing?

Of course I've grown up, of course I'm not a little girl no more. You didn't come, you didn't keep your promise. Soonverysoon, you said. You promised soonverysoon. You promised you would come back to get us, you would come back to see us, but you didn't.

Julia, sweetie, Papá needed me.

We needed you too and don't call me sweetie, you never call me sweetie, why are you calling me sweetie?

Julia, please. I am sorry, I had to be with Papá, poor Papá is so sick.

Papá is a hit man. He is a bad man. Everybody knows that.

Julia, no, you don't understand.

I am not a little girl no more and *I* understand.

We walked all together to Tía's car. We got in. No one said a thing. Mamá was sitting between Willy and me. With one hand she started caressing Willy's head. With the other hand, she caressed mine. She caressed us the way she used to do it, the way we like it. I liked it, but I wanted her to stop and at the same time I wanted her to keep doing it forever.

OCTOBER 18TH

English: Mrs. García
Journal #2

My Weekend
by Julia

This weekend Mamá came to visit us. She doesn't live here, she lives on the other side of the bridge. She lives in Juárez, México. I don't know exactly where she lives because the police took over our house. I guess she lives in the hospital where Papá lies. Papá is a vegetable or something like that. A bullet ran through his head. Mamá is his nurse.

Anyway, Mamá came this weekend and she and Tía took us to the zoo. I had never been to a zoo. It was nice. We liked the monkeys the most, those guys really enjoy life! They hang here and there and yell and laugh and eat all the time. There's nothing wrong going on with their lives. They are just happy to be monkeys. Oh, and when they get mad, they yell at each other, no one tells them not to yell, no one tells them to pretend not to be mad. I wanna be a monkey.

On Sunday we went to see Jonás play soccer. His team lost, but still Tía took us all to eat burgers and fries and chocolate shakes. It was a good weekend.

OCOTBER 24TH

Yesterday we went to church, the regular church, Tía told us to ask God to help Papá get better soon. Even the priest said it at that moment when he asks us to pray for everyone. He said, Lord, we ask you for the recovery of your son Guillermo, protect his wife and his kids, give them strength.

Willy wonders how is it that the priest knows about Papá. I tell him that the priest is like God, he knowsitall. Tía tells me not to say that. She says, The priest doesn't know it all like God. Tía said, I told him, I asked him to pray for your family.

On our way home, Tía tells us that she understands we will miss Mamá now that she's gone back with Papá again, but you must be strong, she says. The Lord is with us, you are not alone. The Lord hears our prayers; the Lord fulfills our needs.

Tonight I will pray to the Lord, and I will tell him to fulfill my need of a normal father and a normal mother. I will ask him to take us back to our old life. I have nothing to lose.

OCTOBER 26TH

Jonás said something interesting today. He was like, you know, if Tío is really a hit man like everyone says, maybe there's some hit man blood in you and in Willy. Wait, no, I don't think Willy has hit man blood, he is too nice, too sweet. He never dares to do anything.

Yeah, Willy is a bit of a coward. Not you, though.

Do you think I can be a hit man? I asked and I could see myself like Mathilda grabbing a gun in that movie.

Mmh, I don't know. Maybe yes, cause the way you kicked Fat Nelly's ass was pretty hit-man-ish.

Oh, yeah it was. And I forgot to write all about it here. But what is there to tell? She was mean to one of the girls in my class that doesn't speak much English. I got mad, I kicked her ass, the end. She is a bully after all, and I hate bullies.

Jonás said everyone in school is still talking about it. Everyone is scared of me. It's best that way, he says. It's better having people scared of you, than people having pity for you.

Do you think people pity me? I asked.

Well…you know, Patty says that people pity kids like us, kids with no dads or moms, kids with sick dads or kids with sick moms. Kids who don't understand a word of English. If you think about it, there are way too many reasons to pity kids in our school.

Jonás' words made me feel sad and sadder. And he noticed it and to cheer me up, he told me he was gonna call Patty so I could tell her myself the story of how I kicked Fat Nelly's ass.

He dialed Patty, and after his Hey, it's me, what's up and stuff, he said, Julia has something to tell you. Yes, about the fight.

I told her, Yeah, so I was there, right? And she was in front of me, then...

OCTOBER 26TH, 9 PM

Maybe Jonás is right. Maybe everyone is right. Maybe there is a reason to be afraid of me. If not…if not…maybe, just maybe, I can create A REASON for people to be AFRAID of me.

Maybe I can be bad, so bad that I will even make the news one day.

One day.

OCTOBER 29TH

Dear Pedro,

Tía says we will see you soon. She says you will take us to see Papá. Willy is very excited. To tell you the truth, I am too. I wanna see Papá.

What we miss the most from Juárez are those tacos we loved, you know what I am talking about, right? Those tacos you used to take us to. We must all go. I want you to drive us past my old school. I wanna say hi. Do you think you can also take us to our old house, I wanna see what's left.

I miss you very very very much.

Julia

P.S. I know you won't get this letter until we finally see each other, but please pretend you got it a long time before that.

NOVEMBER 15TH

A few days ago some of us were tested. They said it was some placement exam or something. Today I was told that, because I got a high grade, I was to be sent to a different class. I tried to convince Mrs. García to please let me stay because I finally have friends here. But she said I will make friends in this other class, and I will get to practice my English more because everyone speaks English there.

But as soon as I got to the other class, I could tell there was no way I was gonna make friends there. I was sure everyone was gonna be white, super-white. In my old class we all know that white kids barely speak with brown kids. I sat in the front row, but to my surprise I wasn't the only brown girl in my class. The only problem was that I chose to sit in the front without thinking, so now everyone probably thinks that I am a nerd. Only nerd kids sit in the front row.

My new teacher is Miss Rogers. She asked me to stand up and introduce myself to the class.

I went, My name is Julia and…and…and I used to live in Juárez, but I don't anymore. I live here in El Paso. I live with my brother, my aunt, my cousin and my bis.

Who? someone asked.

My great-grandmother, but I call her Bis, because great-grandmother in Spanish is bisabuela, and Bis is short for bisabuela. Bisabuela is too long of a word, well, not as long as great-grandmother, I guess…but still…I like short words.

Anyway, what was I saying?

Everyone laughed, even the teacher who said, Let's clap and welcome Julia.

I was so embarrassed. I went back to my seat. Then, it happened. The kid behind me said, Hey, you are the one who kicked Fat Nelly's ass, right?

Yeah, I said.

Hi, my name is Barry.

Barry is so cute.

I might just fall in love.

NOVEMBER 19TH

I don't know what's with Barry, but when we are together
I just feel like talking and talking to him, telling him
everything. Today at lunch he sat with me and told me that his
grandmother on his mom's side was Latina too, from Puerto
Rico. But her parents brought her to the U.S. when she was
just a kid, so she speaks more English than Spanish. She forgot
Spanish a bit. I will never forget Spanish, I told him.

He told me that he just moved to El Paso. He told me that
he and his family move a lot because his dad is in the military. I
am an army brat, he said.

What is that? I asked.

That's what people call kids like me, kids who have to move
a lot because their parents are in the military, he said. He told
me he has lived in Virginia, Georgia, Colorado, and now El Paso.

As I was hearing him, I was thinking of all the places me
and my family lived in before moving to Juárez. I told him,
We have moved a lot too. But I didn't tell him that maybe, just
maybe, we moved a lot because Papá was already with the
narco. I didn't tell him that perhaps I was like him, only I was a
narco brat, not an army brat.

I told Barry that Papá is in the hospital being a vegetable
because he was shot in Juárez.

Is your dad a narco? Barry asked.

I didn't know what to tell him. I thought:

- If I say yes, he might never-ever talk to me again.

- If I say no, he might never-ever talk to me again because he doesn't find me interesting anymore.

So I said, I can't talk about it.
Barry smiled and said, You are cool shit, Julia.

NOVEMBER 19TH, VERY LATE

I am cool shit! He said so. I am. I don't know exactly if that is a compliment or what, but I like the sound of it: COOOOL SHIIIIT.

NOVEMBER 20TH

Today we are crossing the bridge. In the past when we were told that we were crossing the bridge, it meant we were coming to El Paso. Now it means we are going to Juárez. We are crossing by foot because Tía says now it's not as safe to bring her car.

As we walk up to the bridge, we see the Mexican flag, the big green-white-red flag with the eagle in the middle. Willy starts singing the song about the flag, the song that all kids are taught when they're in kindergarten. It says something about sacrificing life and heart for the flag.

Yup, it's kinda corny.

As I hear him singing, I realize that at my new school we don't sing to the flag, we don't do special flag services every Monday in front of the whole school like we do it in México. Well, we do pray to the United States of America, but I haven't learned it all that well.

As soon as we crossed, we saw Pedro.

Pedro, Pedro, Pedro! Willy ran and climbed on top of him.

Pedro looks very skinny. When he saw me he said, How is Miss Julia?

We went to have lunch. He took us to eat turkey tails, Willy's favorite. Pedro and Tía were talking and talking while we ate like the pigs we are.

Are we gonna go to our place? I asked.

Pedro looked at Tía, the way you do when you want her to say yes to something.

We'll see, Tía said. Now it's time to go to the hospital.

Once in the hospital we had to wait for Tía to go see Mamá so she could get a permit for us to go up and see Papá. I don't understand why we have to ask permission to see him. We are his kids!

Hospitals smell funny, like bus stations. They look like a market, they sell everything inside and outside of them: food, magazines, candies, sodas, gums, newspapers. There's people everywhere. People waiting in line, people sitting on the floor, people even sleeping on the floor. People in a good mood and people in a bad mood.

Do you wanna see Papá? Willy asked me.

Well, don't you?

I dunno.

Why?

I'm scared.

Scared of what, Willy?

I dunno, it's just, Jonás said he looked like…

Like…?

Like dead, and I am afraid of the deads.

I too am afraid of the deads, but I didn't say a thing. We both stayed there looking around us.

OK, I want to.

You want to what, Willy?

I want to see him, it's just that it makes me feel scared too.

Are you scared of Papá?

You kidding? I am always scared of Papá.

Well. Now, you shouldn't be. He…he can't do anything. You are safe.

As I said these words to Willy, I was saying them to me too. It's like I am becoming our own mother.

NOVEMBER 21ST

I am having dinner at Barry's, a pre-Thanksgiving dinner, his mother said. She called Tía and so here I am. His mother is funny, she curses a lot like Papá used to, but unlike Papá she is not angry when she says words like *Shit, shitty, goddamn it,* and *fuck.* She used that word a lot while she was cooking. She burned her fingers at least three times while I was there.

Be a lady, Tía had told me. So I offered to help. We all made dinner. I grated the cheese, Barry rinsed the pasta, and his mother prepared the ground beef. She then had a fight with a can opener. She was like, You stupid thing, come on, move, move! We were like a family.

Then his father arrived, Barry calls him Sir. I found that a bit odd. He was like, Yes, sir. No, sir. He made me nervous with his uniform and his boots and everything.

Before we sat down to eat, he changed his clothes, he had shorts and chanclas. He asked me, So Julia, how is El Paso treating you? Do you miss home?

I didn't know what to say, so I only answered, Sometimes.

Barry told us you have moved a lot, just like us.

Yes, I said. You get used to it.

Barry's mom said, In the end, home is where you are. She grabbed her husband's hand, and they kissed. Barry was like, Oh disgusting, why do you have to do that when we are eating? But I thought it was cute.

After dinner, I offered to help with the dishes, but Barry's mom said no, you guys go do whatever. Barry took me to his room, he showed me pictures of all the places he has been.

Moving a lot is not that bad, he said. You get to see many things.

Then it came to me: What if, now that I have a friend, he moves away? I asked him and he said, Maybe, but we will always remain friends, we can write to each other every day if we want to.

I am gonna be torn apart if you leave, I said, and I could feel my face burning hot, embarrassed.

Torn apart? Barry said. Dude, you are indestructible. Nothing can ever tear you apart, remember that.

He began telling me more about all the places his family has been and all the places his father has been sent off.

Has he been in battles? I asked.

Of course, he said. I guess just like your dad, right?

I nodded.

Do you want to talk about *it*, Julia? We don't have to, but if you want… I spent the rest of the afternoon telling Barry about seeing Papá at the hospital and how I can still close my eyes and see him there. He said nothing, he just listened to me patiently.

Barry too is cool shit.

The other day, we had our first Thanksgiving dinner in El Paso. It was nice. We all felt like crying when Tía thanked the Lord for giving her the chance to take care of us. Then she made us pray for Papá's health.

It's been days and I still can't get Papá's face out of my mind. I am glad at the end I was the only one to see him, Willy would have freaked out.

Tía said I had to be quiet. Tía said I had to be a good girl. During all these months, those are the two things Tía has taught me: to be a quiet, good girl.

Papá was there, but it's like he was there only because he was plugged into a bunch of things. He has no hair. His head shines. It was weird, I felt like a mom seeing her baby for the first time in the hospital. Papá was like a baby, he was like an ugly baby. Well, that's what they say about babies when they are born, right? They say just-born babies are ugly. So he looked like a baby, a baby who also happened to be sick.

I still feel the smell on the tip of my nose. It was not just your regular hospital smell. It smelled different, it smelled worse, like pee and poo and something else. It was a smell that clings to your nose and tickles you.

Mamá was there. She was sitting right next to him. She would look at him, she would look at him the same way you look at a baby that you are worried about. She didn't look like Mamá, though. She looked like somebody else. I wonder where Mamá, my real Mamá, is. I wonder where Papá is, my real Papá, not the one looking like an old, sick, ugly baby.

Where are my parents? Who will do the parenting from now on?

DECEMBER 1ST

I read a book accidentally.

OK, I didn't really read the whole book, just a few bits of it here and there.

OK, it was not exactly an accident, because I really did want to read it. But it wasn't mine. It was Miss Rogers'. The name of the book is *Ghostbread*. It's by Sonja Livingston. It sounded spooky and funny at the same time. I found something that I liked, it says:

I loved her beyond words and clothes, and yes beyond even pain. The strangest of things is the way the hungry always return to the very same hand. The hand they know. The one that cannot give.

Mamá's hands cannot give, not anymore. And still, I love her.

DECEMBER 2ND

Barry knows everything about me. He says my life is like a character in *Oliver Twist*. Oliver who? I asked. And then Barry told me the whole story of poor Oliver Twist. I wonder if I have an orphan-kid face.

He said that I had to find out what really happened to Papá. It's your job, he said. He says it is all too fishy, and a person needs the truth. He's right, I need the truth, not the gossip. You need to ask questions, he said, there's nothing worse than a kid who doesn't ask questions. He said he heard that phrase somewhere on TV.

He is right. There's nothing worse than a kid who doesn't ask questions.

DECEMBER 4TH

Pedro called today and said we were horrible parents.

We are what? I asked.

HORRIBLE parents, he said. You came, asked for food, asked for treats and none of you asked about Califas.

Willy was right next to me, holding the phone. He said, Oh, my God, Julia, Califas, we forgot all about Califas!

So it seems Pedro adopted our cat, you know, when what happened, happened. He found him there, a few days after what happened, happened. He was all alone, scared and starving.

So I had to take him home, Pedro said.

You have a home? I asked, surprised.

Well, yes, of course I do, what did you think?

I thought you were ours, I said, just like Califas.

Pedro laughed and laughed. Ay Julia, I miss you so much, he said.

I miss you too, Pedro.

Willy finally left and left me talking to Pedro on the phone. We talked about this and about that. Then I told him I had a big question for him.

You wanna know if the sky is really blue.

No, Pedro, no. This is serious, I said.

You wanna know when will I find a girlfriend.

No, Pedro, no. This is really serious, I said.

OK, shoot, you know you can ask me anything.

What happened to Papá?

Mmhh. Mhhh.

Pedro?

Mmhh. Mhh.

Pedro, tell me.

You know what happened, Julia. It was a stray bullet. You know that is very common here. There are one too many stray bullets.

Pedro?

Julia?

Pedro, you are lying. I know that is not what happened, something else happened. Besides, it wasn't just one bullet, it was way more than one. And what about the police? The police were looking for him.

No, Julia.

Pedro, I am not stupid, stop treating me like I'm stupid. I know, I know the truth, I know you and Papá are bad men. I know you are hit men. I know, I know. I know you two did something very very bad. I know you did something like stealing money, selling drugs and killing people. I know you did something very bad that went very wrong and that is why Willy and I are here, that's why Willy and I are like orphans from a movie waiting for their parents to come back.

Pedro remained silent. He was probably surprised about all I said. I know because I was surprised too. I didn't know I had so many words in me.

Julia, you are not stupid, I know. But you are a kid, you are a little girl who should not know as much as you know. You are a girl who should not have experienced as much as you've experienced. You deserve to know, you deserve much more, but I can't tell you, not now.

He hung up.

DECEMBER 7TH

I found a photo in Tia's house. A photo of my family. From before. A photo in which we look like a happy family. Look like. Were we ever really a happy family? I could not help myself, I grabbed my pencil, I clenched it, and I poked Papá's eyes out. One eye, then the other. Then Mamá's. Don't even look at me, I said.

Then I looked at me, Don't you smile, I said, before poking my eyes out. Then I took the eraser and rubbed my face off. Then Papá's. Then Mamá's.

Gone, we were gone. Like ghosts.

I was about to poke Willy's eyes, but I couldn't. My brother, my baby brother, he is so happy, what does he know? It was then that I started crying.

Look at me, I am still crying, I can't stop. I am crying for Papá. I am crying for Mamá. I am crying for Pedro. I am crying for Willy. I am crying for Califas. I am crying for me, for me, because no one cries for me. I am crying because what the hell.

I am crying because I just fucked up the only photo I had of the family we once were. I am such an idiot.

I am an idiot who can't stop crying.

I am an idiot who loves and hates her mother at the same time.

I am an idiot who loves and hates her father at the same time.

I am an idiot who made her brother cry.

I am an idiot who is just as bad as her parents.

DECEMBER 10TH

Bis says we are all good and bad at the same time. She just says it like that, as if we had all been talking about the depth of life. What did you say, Bis? I asked. She repeats it: We are all good and bad at the same time. Tía adds, yes, that is why our Lord wants us to be clean of sin, to leave the bad behind.

Bis says, No way, José! Then Willy asks, Who is José!? Tía explains that this is just an expression, but she can't seem to explain what it means. We all burst out laughing, even Tía.

So we were all saying, No way, José!— all day long.

Jonás: Julia, can you turn on the TV?

Me: No way, José!

Tía: Willy, can you close the window?

Willy: No way, José!

Me: Tía, are we gonna have your special burgers for dinner?

Tía: No way, José!

We were all laughing and laughing so much that we didn't realize that Bis had gone quiet all day long. Quiet and staring at who knows what. So later that night I heard Tía talking to someone and saying, Maybe you are right, maybe I should send Nana someplace they can take care of her better than we do.

It seems that everytime we seem to be getting somewhere, something pulls us back.

All is good and bad at the same time, I guess.

DECEMBER 13TH

Dear Diary,

I am sorry. I haven't told you that I cheat on you once in a while. Miss Rogers made us start a journal weeks ago, she wants us to write even during our winter break, which is soon. She says that we have to write every single day of our lives in them. This is called journaling. And we all have to be journaling about everything that happens to us, what we think about school, home, the street, our families, our friends, and the holidays.

Everyone in class was complaining. No Miss, it will be difficult, some said. Not me. I have no problem with writing and you know it. I will write even more. I will write everything that I see, hear, smell, taste, touch, live, dream.

E v e r y t h i n g

But it is not the same. I am not able to write in the new journal the same way I've written here. It will never be the same, first of all because in the new one, I'll have to write in English.

And, second, because Miss Rogers will be reading everything.

Don't worry, Diary, I still love you the best. I am going to make the other journal think I love it, I'm going to write emotions I don't really have but that hopefully will make me get a couple A's. And I want those A's.

Really, Diary, you have nothing to worry about. You are my favorite, you understand me the most. You are the only one who really knows me. You know me and my feelings and my words and my ideas and my drawings and my everything.

My everything.

DECEMBER 14TH

Barry borrowed Miss Rogers' book, the one I accidentally read. Well, I didn't read it, I just skimmed it. But he is reading the whole book. He says it is about a girl who reminds him of me. She is all alone, her mom is there, but she is not there, she is very poor, and she has no dad. I am not trying to be mean, Barry said at the end.

I know he wasn't trying to be mean. I know he is right. I am a bit like the girl from *Ghostbread*. Her name is Sonja. There's a part where Sonja says that parents are like ghosts...

Papá is a ghost. He is a ghost that floats around Mamá. He floats around me. He floats around Willy. Papá is a killer ghost, he is the ghost of a bad man who did bad things. He killed people, men, women, kids...kids? Did Papá kill kids too?

I don't like to imagine Papá killing people, but lately I can't help it. I dream of him shooting, killing people. Papá running around the city shooting and shooting. Papá driving the car el Gringo or la Comadreja or both gave him. Papá shooting and shooting. Until he gets home, just like any other dad. He kisses his wife, his kids, he washes his hands and asks, What's for dinner?

Papá is a murderer, but we don't know it. Papá is a murderer who takes his kids for ice cream, just like any other dad.

Bis is way worse. The things she says either make no sense or make complete sense. There's no happy medium, like Tía says.

Take today, for example. The news in the papers and on the TV is that many, many dead bodies were found in a pit. Tía said, That happens everywhere, not only here, why do they make that big a deal of it?

That's exactly the problem, Bis said, that we hear about it so much, that they do this so many times, that we end up wondering what's the big deal, forgetting it is *actually* a big deal.

Willy: What's the big deal?

Tía: Nothing.

Bis: People die every day in horrible ways.

Willy: Papá DIED?

Tía: You see? You are scaring the boy.

Bis: Your Papá was already dead.

Tía: Ay, Nana.

Willy leaves directly to his Legos. That's his thing, playing with Legos when he doesn't understand grown-up conversations. Sometimes I don't understand grown-up conversations either, but I pretend I do. Sometimes I even try to add something or ask questions. But when I say something, they laugh, and when I ask something, they don't say a thing.

Me: Why did you say Papá was already dead, Bis?

Tía: You see? Now you are scaring Julia, Nana.

Bis: The truth is this, Julia. It is best to die an honorable man.

DECEMBER 18TH

Everybody in school says that Fat Nelly has promised to take revenge before classes are over. I asked Barry, Classes over today, or when? He had no answer, but I better be prepared.

Barry says I should not be scared, he says that if I did it once, I can do it again and again and again. Plus, you are not alone anymore, Barry says.

Jonás says the same thing, he says I have nothing to worry about. He says that I can just tell her and everyone else who my dad is. Once they know you are the daughter of a famous hit man, no one will touch you.

Well, but the hit man ended up in the hospital, how can they be afraid of him?

No, dumbass, you don't tell them to be afraid of your dad, but to be afraid of YOU.

Afraid of me? Why would anyone be afraid of me?

Because you are his daughter and you have his blood, you are like him.

Like him?

I say nothing in my first period.

I say nothing in my second period.

I say nothing at lunch.

I say nothing for a long while.

When I arrive, I tell Tía my stomach has been acting weird, like a pain that comes and goes, I say. I wanna go to bed.

Just for the record, I wasn't lying, my stomach did hurt but I was too busy saying nothing and thinking about Fat Nelly.

Tía says to take a shower.

I do what I'm told.

I look at myself in the bathroom mirror. I am the daughter of a hit man, I tell the mirror. And before I know it, the pain is back. I sit down on the toilet, I pee, but the pain doesn't go away.

When I wipe I see there's blood, I am bleeding, bleeding. Tía, Tía I am bleeding, I yell. Tía came right away, she covered me with a towel and hugged me close. She said I had nothing to worry about, she said I wasn't sick, she said I was becoming a woman.

A woman.

And this woman is the daughter of a hit man. It's in my blood.

DECEMBER 26TH

Dear Diary,

I haven't seen you in so long, right? So much has happened, I don't even know how to start.

Let's see. Papá died. We missed the last day of classes and stayed in Juárez for a few days.

We had to have a funeral and everything. No one came. It was only Mamá, Tía, Pedro, Jonás, Bis, Willy and me.

Willy and Mamá cried the most.

I cried too, but I also tried to keep it together. I don't even know why.

Papá is now buried in Juárez, like everything we had. Once we were done, Tía insisted we eat over there in the place that Papá liked the most. Everyone looked at us, like they knew who we were and who we were mourning. Or maybe not, maybe it was just my imagination.

We said goodbye to Pedro, and I felt that this time it was really a goodbye. I don't think we are seeing him anytime soon. He hugged every one of us but me. It's like he was scared of me or something. I am gonna miss you, Julia, he said. I should have told him I was gonna miss him too. It's like that day that Papá, all drunk, asked me if I loved him, and I said nothing. I just stared at him like I stared at Pedro when he said goodbye. Feeling but not feeling.

Papá died and with him a little piece of me died too, the piece that hated him, that died. Papá died and with him a big part of our life died too and that part included Pedro.

On our way back to El Paso, Mamá was all quiet, I wonder what part of her died with Papá.

DECEMBER 28TH

We obviously did not celebrate Christmas this year. Since Papá's funeral, Mamá has been in bed. It's like she walked into our room and had no intention of ever coming out.

Tía takes her these shakes with vitamins and shit. If you don't eat, at least drink this to be strong, Tía tells Mamá.

Mamá is all silence. She stares at the ceiling like Bis stares at who knows what when she is out of herself.

But Bis is now all herself, it's like all of a sudden she is not forgetting who she is and who we are. She goes and sits next to Mamá and holds her hand. She says, This too shall pass, mija.

Mamá looks like Papá when he was in the hospital—there, but not there.

JANUARY 2ND

New year, new life.

Tomorrow we all go back to our lives. Tía will go back to work, and we will go back to school. She has had to tell again and again the story of her brother-in-law who died and how she has had to take care of everything and everybody.

Tomorrow I go back to Barry and Fat Nelly, and I will have to pretend I am OK. Maybe some of my classmates already know what happened, and they will come to me and say, I am sorry for your loss. What does that even mean?!

But the truth is, I am really the one who is sorry for MY loss.

JANUARY 11TH

Mamá gets out of bed once in a while. She goes and makes coffee. She goes and smokes a cigarette. She goes and makes a soup or a sandwich for Willy or Jonás or me, and then she goes back to bed.

She talks to no one. She showers every other day. She stays in bed most of the time.

Willy and me are really like orphans now. Willy and I don't have a dad, a mom, a house, or a country.

We have nothing.

That's what I tell Barry: My brother and I, we have nothing now. Barry laughs, which makes me very angry at first.

Are you crazy? he says. You have many things. Before I am able to open my mouth and say, No, I don't, he goes and makes a list for me.

JANUARY 12TH

List of things I have according to Barry:

- Your tía.
- Your cousin.
- Me, Barry.
- Your cousin's almost girlfriend, Patty.
- Your Bis.
- Me.
- Your brother.
- Me.
- Your Mamá.
- Me.
- Your new school, your new neighborhood, your new city.
- Me.

Then he adds, You probably don't believe me now, but you will. It might take time, but one day you will realize that you have way more than you think, way more than many people here.

JANUARY 17TH

Today, when I arrived home from school, Bis was outside, sitting on a chair on the porch. She was singing a song about a woman who cries and cries. But it was not a sad song. It wasn't happy either. It was just…I don't know…nice and sweet.

I sat on the floor right next to Bis' feet. She was wearing socks with sandals. But that's not because Bis is sick and doesn't know what she is doing. Really, she wore those even before she got sick.

It seemed at first that Bis did not even notice that I was there, but then she grabbed my hair, she undid my ponytail and without pausing in her song, she started braiding my hair. A light breeze crossed my face. I closed my eyes and allowed myself to feel.

The lyrics of the happy-sad song made my eyes tear, but at the same time, the air, that cool, beautiful air, made me smile. It's like being happy and sad at the same time. Happy and sad.

All of a sudden, Willy yelled, Migra, migra, miiiiigra! It brought me back from wherever I was. He was on the street running around with some other kids, being chased by Jonás. They were all laughing and excited about the game. Willy, playing on the street, like he had always wanted. Like we had always wanted, but we couldn't because back then, back home, it was too dangerous. Look at him now. Who would have believed this was even possible?

We both have so much now, after all.

Sad and happy, I say out loud. Good and bad.

Bis, yells Willy from the street, do you want to play with us? Do you want to be the migra now?

No way, José! she yells back.

She goes back to singing and braiding my hair. She pulls a bit too hard, but it's OK, I don't mind, it sometimes has to hurt for a braid to look pretty.

JANUARY 22ND

Today I went grocery shopping with my tía. Mamá came along, I think it was the first time she's gone out with us since, you know.

We went to that old store in downtown, the one on Stanton Street. I like going there—one, because they sell stuff that I really like, but two, because from there you can see beyond the border, beyond the bridge.

From there, you can see it all. If you look ahead, you can see the city that we left behind. If you look back, you see the city we now live in.

So I did.

I saw Juárez.

I saw El Paso.

Juárez.

El Paso.

Two places that are really one bridge apart. Two places that are one.

I closed my eyes for a second and I saw...I saw everything, my whole life like in a movie.

First I felt like crying. But then I thought, If it wasn't for that, I wouldn't be here, and yes, I will always miss the life I had before. The good parts and even the bad parts, because that is all part of the whole, and you can't separate them. Like these cities, you can never separate them, there will always be a bridge.

Julia, let's go, says Tía.

I tell myself the same: Julia, let's go.

Julia, are you OK? asks Mamá who is now by my side. It's like she understands what I am doing, because she puts her arm around my shoulders and we stand there, just watching. It might take time, she says. And I don't understand what exactly she means at first.

But then I do. Isn't that what Barry told me?

It's like when I start writing an entry in my diary, I don't know where it will take me and then, when I start getting close to the last paragraph, I'm there, I get it. I'm crossing a bridge.

So, yes, it might take time, but one day I will realize what I've got.

The everything. My everything.

ACKNOWLEDGMENTS

This book was first written in Spanish. When I decided to translate it, I received wonderful advice from Andrea Beltrán and Yasmin Ramirez, thank you both. When I realized translation was impossible and rewrote it all over again in English, John Pluecker provided words, love, support, and more love to make it possible, gracias hermano mío. These pages owe everything they are now to Jessica Powers, Jill Bell, Lee and Bobby Byrd, Stephanie Frescas Macías, Mary Fountaine. Thank you, thank you, thank you.

CPSIA information can be obtained
at www.ICGtesting.com
Printed in the USA
LVHW111331211219
641293LV00001BE/1/P

9 781947 627178